WORKI
WITH
NUMBERS

AUTHOR
James T. Shea

CONSULTANT
Susan L. Beutel
Consulting/Resource Teacher
Lamoille North Supervisory Union, VT

ACKNOWLEDGEMENTS

Senior Math Editor: Karen L. Lassiter

Project Coordinator: Cynthia Ellis

Project Design and Development:
The Wheetley Company

Cover Design: Robin Bouvette
Cover Illustration: Danal Terry

WORKING WITH NUMBERS SERIES:

Level A/Point	Level D/Rectangle	Consumer
Level B/Line	Level E/Pentagon	Refresher
Level C/Triangle	Level F/Hexagon	Algebra

STECK-VAUGHN
COMPANY
ELEMENTARY • SECONDARY • ADULT • LIBRARY

ISBN: 0-8114-4237-3

TABLE OF CONTENTS

Unit 1 • Working with Whole Numbers

Place Value 4
Reading and Writing Numbers 5
Comparing and Ordering 6
Rounding 7
Addition of Whole Numbers 8-9
Problem-Solving Strategy:
  Use Logic 10-11
Subtraction 12-13
Addition of 3 or More Numbers. . . 14
Problem Solving—Applications . . . 15
Problem-Solving Strategy:
  Identify Extra Information. . . . 16-17
Addition and Subtraction of
  Larger Numbers. 18
Estimation of Sums and
  Differences 19
Problem Solving—Applications . . . 20
Unit 1 Review. 21

Unit 2 • Multiplication

1-digit Numbers. 22
Problem Solving—Applications . . . 23
2-digit by 2-digit Numbers 24-25
3-digit by 2-digit Numbers 26
Zeros in Multiplication 27
Problem-Solving Strategy:
  Use a Table 28-29
Estimation of Products 30
Problem Solving—Applications . . . 31
3-digit Numbers by
  3-digit Numbers. 32-33
Problem-Solving Strategy:
  Choose an Operation 34-35
Large Numbers 36
Unit 2 Review. 37

Unit 3 • Division

1-digit Divisors 38
Problem Solving—Applications . . . 39
1-digit Divisors with
  Remainders 40-41
Problem-Solving Strategy:
  Make a Drawing 42-43

Zeros in Quotients 44
2-digit Divisors: Multiples of 10 . . . 45
Problem Solving—Applications . . . 46
Trial Quotients: Too Large or
  Too Small 47
2-digit Divisors 48-49
Problem-Solving Strategy:
  Choose an Operation 50-51
Estimating Quotients 52
Unit 3 Review. 53

Unit 4 • Working with Fractions

Meaning of Fractions 54-55
Equivalent Fractions. 56
Comparing and Ordering
  Fractions 57
Equivalent Fractions in
  Higher Terms 58
Equivalent Fractions in
  Simplest Terms 59
Improper Fractions and Mixed
  Numbers 60-61
Addition and Subtraction of Fractions
  with Like Denominators. 62-63
Problem-Solving Strategy:
  Find a Pattern. 64-65
Problem Solving—Applications . . . 66
Addition and Subtraction of
  Mixed Numbers with
  Like Denominators 67
Addition of Fractions with Different
  Denominators. 68-69
Subtraction of Fractions with
  Different Denominators 70-71
Problem-Solving Strategy:
  Work Backwards 72-73
Problem Solving—Applications . . . 74
Unit 4 Review 75

Unit 5 • Fractions and Measurement

Addition of Mixed Numbers with
  Different Denominators 76-77
Addition of Mixed Numbers with
  Regrouping 78-79

Subtraction of Mixed Numbers with
Different Denominators 80-81
Subtraction of Fractions and
Mixed Numbers From
Whole Numbers. 82-83
Subtraction of Mixed Numbers with
Regrouping 84-85
Problem-Solving Strategy:
Use Guess and Check. 86-87
Problem Solving—Applications . . . 88
Customary Length. 89
Customary Weight. 90
Customary Capacity. 91
Problem Solving—Applications . . 92-93
Problem-Solving Strategy:
Use a Formula 94-95
Unit 5 Review. 96-97

Unit 6 • Working with Decimals

Meaning of Decimals 98
Decimal Place Value. 99
Reading and Writing Decimals . 100-101
Compare and Order Decimals. . 102-103
Problem-Solving Strategy:
Make a List 104-105
Problem Solving—Applications . . . 106
Rounding Decimals 107

Problem-Solving Strategy:
Use Estimation 108-109
Fraction and Decimal Equivalents . . 110
Fraction and Decimal Equivalents . . 111
Problem Solving—Applications . . . 112
Unit 6 Review. 113

Unit 7 • Decimals and Measurement

Addition of Decimals 114-116
Estimation of Decimal Sums. 117
Subtraction of Decimals 118-119
Estimation of Decimal
Differences 120
Problem Solving—Applications . . . 121
Problem-Solving Strategy:
Use a Graph 122-123
Metric Length:
Meter and Kilometer 124
Metric Length:
Centimeter and Millimeter 125
Metric Mass 126
Metric Capacity 127
Relating Units 128
Changing Units 129
Problem-Solving Strategy:
Select a Strategy. 130
Unit 7 Review. 131-132

Final Review

Final Review 133-136

Place Value

A place-value chart can help you understand whole numbers.
Each digit in a number has a value based on its place in
the number.

The 7 is in the millions place.
Its value is 7 millions or 7,000,000.

The 5 is in the ten thousands place.
Its value is 5 ten thousands or 50,000.

The 3 is in the hundreds place.
Its value is 3 hundreds or 300.

hundred millions	ten millions	millions	hundred thousands	ten thousands	thousands	hundreds	tens	ones
		7	6	5	4	3	2	1

PRACTICE

Write each number in the place-value chart.

1. 366,789,302
2. 2,304,361
3. 19,076,541
4. 8,854,632
5. 97,065
6. 8,005,002

	hundred millions	ten millions	millions	hundred thousands	ten thousands	thousands	hundreds	tens	ones
1.	3	6	6	7	8	9	3	0	2
2.									
3.									
4.									
5.									
6.									

Write the place name for the 5 in each number.

a *b*

7. 362,050 ___tens___   2,250,876 _____

8. 219,572,080 _____   5,712,309 _____

9. 876,529 _____   1,804,075 _____

10. 15,782 _____   53,047,260 _____

Write the value of the underlined digit.

a *b*

11. 1,39<u>0</u>,526 ___0 thousands___   207,3<u>8</u>9 _____

12. 9<u>8</u>3,576,091 _____   <u>4</u>,523,551 _____

13. <u>4</u>50,086 _____   232,87<u>5</u> _____

14. <u>1</u>72,034,056 _____   67,<u>0</u>43 _____

Reading and Writing Numbers

Comiskey Park and Wrigley Field are baseball stadiums in Chicago. The two stadiums together hold about 81,960 people.

We read and write this number as: eighty-one thousand, nine hundred sixty.

The digit 8 means 8 ten thousands, or 80,000.

The digit 1 means 1 thousand, or 1000.

The digit 9 means 9 hundreds, or 900.

The digit 6 means 6 tens, or 60.

The digit 0 means 0 ones, or 0.

Notice that commas are used to separate the digits into groups of three. This helps make larger numbers easier to read.

hundred millions	ten millions	millions	hundred thousands	ten thousands	thousands	hundreds	tens	ones
				8	1,	9	6	0
Millions			Thousands			Ones		

Rewrite each number. Insert commas where needed.

	a	*b*	*c*
1.	758493 _758,493_	6473829 _____	868582 _____
2.	2030200 _____	5000400 _____	6050407 _____
3.	30782 _____	406702 _____	3908454 _____

Write each number using digits. Insert commas where needed.

4. seven hundred twenty thousand, four hundred sixty-two _____ _720,462_

5. twenty-five thousand, two hundred one _____

6. one hundred eighty-four thousand, thirty-nine _____

7. one hundred million, two hundred forty-three thousand _____

8. two hundred ten thousand, six hundred twelve _____

9. ten million, two hundred seventy-five _____

Write each number in words. Insert commas where needed.

10. 16,349 _sixteen thousand, three hundred forty-nine_

11. 776 _____

12. 16 _____

13. 123,456 _____

Comparing and Ordering

To compare two numbers, begin at the left.
Compare the digits in each place.
The symbol > means "is greater than." $3 > 2$
The symbol < means "is less than." $5 < 10$
The symbol = means "is equal to." $6 = 6$

Compare 63 and 55.

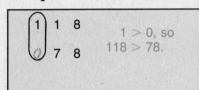

6   3
5   5   6 > 5, so
          63 > 55.

Compare 118 and 78.

1   1   8
    7   8   1 > 0, so
             118 > 78.

Compare 237 and 263.

2   3   7   The hundreds
              digits are the
2   6   3   same. Compare
              the tens digits.
3 < 6, so 237 < 263.

PRACTICE

Compare. Write <, >, or =.

	a		b		c
1. 56 __<__ 65		95 _____ 90		95 _____ 100	
2. 34 _____ 80		123 _____ 213		109 _____ 106	
3. 80 _____ 80		206 _____ 108		309 _____ 1007	
4. 1005 _____ 399		865 _____ 79		2020 _____ 2100	
5. 702 _____ 7001		434 _____ 343		927 _____ 927	
6. 6250 _____ 3199		2049 _____ 1909		4987 _____ 2007	
7. 93,000 _____ 93,001		79,160 _____ 79,162		46,000 _____ 45,999	

Write in order from least to greatest.

8. 23   32   27 ___ _23_   _27_   _32_ _____

9. 345   534   453 _____

10. 258   635   335 _____

11. 255   982   109 _____

12. 91   190   119 _____

13. 956   665   596 _____

14. 764   628   123 _____

15. 486   914   800 _____

16. 3155   6208   2542 _____

Rounding

Rounded numbers tell about how many. You can use a number line to help you round numbers.

Remember, when a number is halfway, always round the number up.

Round 32 to the nearest ten.

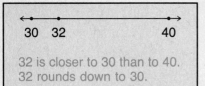

30 32   40

32 is closer to 30 than to 40.
32 rounds down to 30.

Round 650 to the nearest hundred.

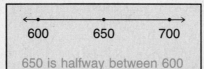

600   650   700

650 is halfway between 600 and 700.
650 rounds up to 700.

Round 2674 to the nearest hundred.

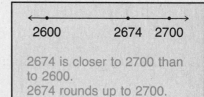

2600   2674 2700

2674 is closer to 2700 than to 2600.
2674 rounds up to 2700.

PRACTICE

Round to the nearest ten.

	a	b	c	d
1.	48 __50__	73 _____	39 _____	25 _____
2.	54 _____	62 _____	86 _____	41 _____

Round to the nearest hundred.

	a	b	c	d
3.	361 __400__	629 _____	750 _____	299 _____
4.	892 _____	567 _____	228 _____	117 _____
5.	539 _____	149 _____	683 _____	450 _____

Round to the nearest hundred.

	a	b	c	d
6.	3547 __3500__	3499 _____	7305 _____	1778 _____
7.	9672 _____	7829 _____	2230 _____	9563 _____
8.	19,205 __19,200__	33,284 _____	54,645 _____	11,921 _____

Addition

To add, start with the digits in the ones place.
Regroup as needed.

Find: 796 + 304

	Add the ones. Regroup.	Add the tens. Regroup.	Add the hundreds. Regroup.

Add the ones. Regroup.

Th	H	T	O
		1	
	7	9	6
+	3	0	4
			0

Add the tens. Regroup.

Th	H	T	O
	1	*1*	
	7	9	6
+	3	0	4
		0	0

Add the hundreds. Regroup.

Th	H	T	O
1	*1*	*1*	
	7	9	6
+	3	0	4
1	*1*	0	0

GUIDED PRACTICE

Add.

	a	*b*	*c*	*d*

1.

Th	H	T	O
	1		
	4	5	0
+	3	9	4
	8	4	4

Th	H	T	O
	2	5	1
+	3	6	6

Th	H	T	O
	5	5	8
+	6	4	5

Th	H	T	O
	7	1	2
+	6	7	8

2.

Th	H	T	O
	3	9	4
+	7	5	9

Th	H	T	O
	6	5	4
+	5	0	6

Th	H	T	O
	4	3	1
+	6	8	7

Th	H	T	O
	7	5	0
+	9	4	7

3.

Th	H	T	O
	1	*1*	
	6	3	9
+		8	2
	7	2	1

Th	H	T	O
		4	6
+	5	6	7

Th	H	T	O
	8	2	6
+		7	9

Th	H	T	O
		3	5
+	8	0	6

4.

Th	H	T	O
		9	7
+	3	4	4

Th	H	T	O
	5	3	2
+		1	9

Th	H	T	O
	6	0	5
+		5	6

Th	H	T	O
	4	9	3
+		2	8

Add.

	a	b	c	d	e
1.	546 +277	458 +385	267 + 49	193 +239	529 +433
2.	94 +407	296 +302	81 +319	573 +241	345 + 83
3.	946 +304	381 + 19	476 +843	35 +781	643 + 65
4.	623 +947	718 +468	503 + 57	764 + 58	432 +379
5.	265 +555	69 +248	924 +618	645 +478	576 +367

Line up the digits. Then add.

	a	b	c
6.	55 + 982 = _____	486 + 14 = _____	543 + 862 = _____

	a	b	c
7.	984 + 587 = _____	772 + 877 = _____	165 + 65 = _____

◈ MIXED PRACTICE ▬▬▬▬▬

Write the value of the underlined digit.

	a	b
1.	3,078,921 _____	4,512,073 _____

Compare. Write <, >, or =.

	a	b	c	d
2.	289 _____ 298	307 _____ 370	6209 _____ 3678	846 _____ 846

9

PROBLEM-SOLVING STRATEGY

Use Logic

Some problems can be solved using logic. Using logic is like using clues to solve a mystery. First, read the problem and look for clues. Then, make a list or chart or draw pictures to help you keep track of the clues. Next, solve the problem.

Read the problem.

Joe, Wong, and Rafael go to the same school. One walks, one rides the school bus, and one gets a ride from his father. Joe does not use any vehicle. Wong's father does not have a car. Who walks, who rides the bus, and who gets a ride from his father?

Look for clues.

Clue 1. Joe does not use a vehicle.
Clue 2. Wong's father does not have a car.

Make a chart.

Fill in the chart using the clues you have found.

	Walks	Father's car	School bus
Joe	YES	no	no
Wong	no	no	YES
Rafael	no	YES	no

Solve the problem.

Joe walks.
Wong rides the bus.
Rafael rides with his father.

Use logic to solve each problem.

1. Jessica, Tim, and Jeff have pets. One has a dog, one has a canary, and one has a goldfish. Jessica is a friend of the boy who has the dog. Tim's pet is a goldfish. Who has the canary?

   Clue 1. Jessica is a friend of the boy who has the dog.
   Clue 2. Tim's pet is a goldfish.

	dog	goldfish	canary
Jessica			
Tim			
Jeff			

   Answer _____

2. Yoko, James, and Elsa were the three winners of the relay race. James was not first. Elsa finished between the other two. Who was first? Who was second? Who was third?

   first _____

   second _____

   third _____

3. Jerry, Larry, and Harry each have 1 younger child in their family. Together, the boys' families include 2 sisters and one brother. Larry does not have a sister. Which ones have sisters? Who has a brother?

   brother _____

   sister _____

   sister _____

4. April, Sue, Juanita, and Kay each belong to a different team. One is on the swim team, one is on the basketball team, one is on the track team, and one plays football. Juanita and Kay are afraid of the water. Sue forgot her helmet at last week's practice. Kay broke a record for the 100-meter dash. Which person is on which team?

   swim team _____

   basketball team _____

   track team _____

   football team _____

Subtraction

To subtract, start with the digits in the ones place.
Regroup as needed.

Find: 836 − 449

Subtract the ones. Regroup.	Subtract the tens. Regroup.	Subtract the hundreds.
| ```
  H  T  O
     2 16
  8  3̶  6̶
− 4  4  9
─────────
        7
``` | ```
     12
  H  2̶  O
  7     16
  8̶  3̶  6̶
− 4  4  9
─────────
     8  7
``` | ```
     12
  H  2̶  O
  7     16
  8̶  3̶  6̶
− 4  4  9
─────────
  3  8  7
``` |

GUIDED PRACTICE

Subtract.

 a   *b*   *c*   *d*

1.

H	T	O		H	T	O		H	T	O		H	T	O
7	12 2̶	13												
8̶	3̶	3̶		6	9	2		5	9	2		6	9	1
−2	8	7		−1	1	8		−3	4	5		−2	8	8
5	4	6												

2.

H	T	O		H	T	O		H	T	O		H	T	O
8	3 4̶	17 7		9	6	8		9	7	6		9	3	2
−1	3	8		−6	5	9		−6	1	7		−8	2	9
7	0	9												

3.

H	T	O		H	T	O		H	T	O		H	T	O
1	9 10 10̶	10 0̶												
2̶	0̶	0̶		4	9	3		9	0	6		3	1	8
−	3	5		−	6	2		−	3	2		−	6	6
1	6	5												

4.

H	T	O		H	T	O		H	T	O		H	T	O
8	16 6̶	14 4̶												
9̶	7̶	4̶		6	1	2		7	7	1		5	6	0
−8	8	5		−5	1	3		−3	4	9		−	9	1
0	8	9												
```

Subtract.

	a	*b*	*c*	*d*	*e*
1.	7 8 2 −2 3 9	3 8 2 − 7 3	9 2 6 − 3 8	6 3 5 −2 8 9	3 6 4 −2 7 8
2.	5 0 0 −3 1 3	7 1 4 −3 2 6	8 2 3 − 5 6	6 1 3 −4 2 2	5 2 7 −2 4 7
3.	3 4 5 − 2 9	8 2 3 − 2 4	9 2 0 − 8 8	5 1 0 − 6 7	6 2 3 − 8 2
4.	8 4 5 −1 5 4	7 4 2 − 3 6	3 8 6 − 7 4	1 2 1 − 4 3	8 3 5 −6 8 1

Line up the digits. Then subtract.

    a   *b*   *c*

5. 690 − 413 = _____   780 − 341 = _____   855 − 436 = _____

  690
 −413

6. 136 − 65 = _____   299 − 43 = _____   777 − 84 = _____

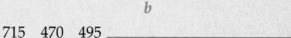

MIXED PRACTICE

Write in order from least to greatest.

     a   *b*

1. 36 53 14 _____   715 470 495 _____

Line up the digits. Then add.

    a   *b*   *c*

2. 226 + 720 = _____   449 + 855 = _____   952 + 638 = _____

Addition of 3 or More Numbers

To add three or more numbers, use the same steps as when adding two numbers.

Find: 949 + 753 + 531

Add the ones. Regroup.	Add the tens. Regroup.	Add the hundreds. Regroup.

```
  Th H T O              Th H T O              Th H T O
        1                    1 1                 2  1 1
     9  4 9                9  4 9                9  4 9
     7  5 3                7  5 3                7  5 3
  +  5  3 1             +  5  3 1             +  5  3 1
          3                    3 3              2  2 3 3
```

PRACTICE

Add.

	a	b	c	d	e
1.	1 2 2 5 6 2 4 9 +1 5 7 —— 6 6 2	4 1 9 6 1 7 +3 1 4 ——	1 1 5 2 8 7 +3 7 9 ——	2 3 8 1 8 6 +3 4 7 ——	3 9 2 7 4 7 +7 4 1 ——
2.	3 0 4 8 6 +1 8 8 ——	3 9 6 8 + 1 9 ——	9 8 1 0 6 +3 0 7 ——	2 5 9 0 +2 0 8 ——	1 0 5 6 2 + 7 ——
3.	1 2 1 3 1 1 7 2 3 4 +5 2 5 —— 1 0 8 9	5 5 9 3 0 4 2 0 5 +1 9 8 ——	4 3 8 1 6 0 6 3 8 +1 0 6 ——	7 1 8 1 6 4 1 3 0 +6 0 7 ——	2 6 5 3 2 2 6 7 4 +4 3 9 ——

Line up the digits. Then add.

a	b

4. 149 + 753 + 531 = _____   489 + 189 + 78 = _____

```
  149
  753
 +531
 ————
```

PROBLEM SOLVING

Applications

Write each number using words.

1. The moon is 406,699 kilometers from the earth.

Answer _____

_____

2. One Pacific-type locomotive weighs 288,600 pounds.

Answer _____

_____

3. During one year there were 3,909,000 births in the United States.

Answer _____

_____

4. In the same year, 1,519,000 persons died in the United States.

Answer _____

_____

5. The pilot on a jet plane told the passengers that they were flying at an altitude of 32,000 feet.

Answer _____

_____

6. The planet Mars is 227,700,000 kilometers from the earth.

Answer _____

_____

Write each number using digits.

7. The football stadium can hold seventy-five thousand, four hundred people.

Answer _____

8. The satellite orbited the earth at a speed of over seventeen thousand five hundred miles per hour.

Answer _____

9. Indiana has one hundred forty-six thousand, one hundred sixty-nine acres of national forest land.

Answer _____

10. The nearest the moon comes to the earth is two hundred twenty-one thousand, four hundred sixty-three miles.

Answer _____

11. The population of the United States is about two hundred forty-four million.

Answer _____

12. The Statue of Liberty weighs two hundred four thousand kilograms.

Answer _____

PROBLEM-SOLVING STRATEGY

Identify Extra Information

Some problems may include more facts than you need to solve the problem. Often you must read the problem several times to decide which facts are needed and which facts are extras. Crossing out extra facts can help you solve the problem. Use the remaining facts to solve the problem.

Read the problem.

> Ramon has saved $42. He wants to buy a pair of ice skates. A new pair of skates costs $35. A used pair costs $15. How much more does a new pair cost than a used pair?

Decide which facts are needed.

> A new pair of ice skates costs $35.
> A used pair costs $15.

Decide which facts are extra.

> Ramon has saved $42.

Solve the problem.

> $35 − $15 = $20

In each problem, cross out the extra facts. Then solve the problem.

1. Judy worked 3 hours on Monday, 2 hours on Wednesday, and ~~will work 6 hours on Saturday~~. How many hours did she work in all on Monday and Wednesday?

Answer _____

2. John lives 4 miles from school. Saturday he rode his bike 2 miles to the park. He rode 3 miles around the bike path there, and then rode his bike home again. How far did he ride his bike?

Answer _____

3. Pablo bought a car that cost $950 and paid $50 in sales tax. Edna bought a car that cost $1275 and paid $65 in sales tax. How much tax did Pablo and Edna pay together?

Answer _____

4. Jim earns $50 a week. In three weeks, he put $25, $35, and $30 into his savings account. How much did Jim put into his savings account during those three weeks?

Answer _____

5. Renee earned $15 mowing lawns last weekend. This weekend she earned $23. Last week she bought a cassette tape for $8. How much more money did she earn this weekend than last weekend?

Answer _____

6. Odetta saved $35. She bought a new sweatshirt for $12. She is now saving the rest for a computer game that costs $20. How much money does she have left?

Answer _____

7. Joseph is 62 inches tall and weighs 98 pounds. Alice is 60 inches tall and weighs 88 pounds. How much do they weigh altogether?

Answer _____

8. Ralph's new bike cost $98. He added a light that cost $15. Ralph earned $18 a week delivering papers to pay for his bike. How much did Ralph spend for the bike and light together?

Answer _____

9. Carol has saved $45. May has saved $30. Carol and May went shopping with their saved money. Carol bought a new dress for $35. May did not buy anything. How much money does Carol have left?

Answer _____

10. Marcus worked 40 hours last week and earned $200. This week he will work 30 hours and earn $150. How many hours will he have worked in all?

Answer _____

11. Wanda works 15 hours a week and earns $90. Her friend Alonzo works 20 hours a week and earns $100. What is the total number of hours Wanda and Alonzo together work in a week?

Answer _____

12. Sumi lives 7 miles from school. He rides the bus 35 minutes to go to school. It takes Sumi 40 minutes to go home from school because the bus takes a different route. How many minutes does it take Sumi to ride the bus to and from school?

Answer _____

Addition and Subtraction of Larger Numbers

To add or subtract larger numbers, start with the ones digits.
Regroup as needed.

PRACTICE

Add.

	a	b	c	d
1.	*1 1 1 1* 3 8,9 1 7 +6 1,1 9 7 *1 0 0,1 1 4*	5 6,4 5 9 +4 6,5 5 4	6 7,9 4 3 +9 0,4 9 8	6,7 5 8 +6 3,2 8 4
2.	6 3,4 5 8 +2 6,4 0 8	6,4 0 8 +2 3,5 0 2	7 2 4 +4 3,2 7 9	3 6,1 0 6 +2 3,9 0 4
3.	1 9,7 8 9 + 2 1 9	9 4,3 8 7 + 5 8 9	1 7,0 0 0 + 2,0 0 0	1 8,5 5 4 + 4 4 6

Subtract.

	a	b	c	d
4.	*15 12 11* *3 5 2 1 15* 4 6,3 2 5 −1 7,8 5 8 *2 8,4 6 7*	5 6,4 5 2 −2 7,5 6 4	4 5,3 8 4 −1 7,5 9 6	6 3,3 3 8 −2 7,9 4 9
5.	6 0,9 8 0 −4 1,9 9 1	4 0,7 0 6 −2 1,8 5 7	5 0,0 0 4 −2 3,5 7 9	7 9,0 0 5 −2 9,0 0 8
6.	7 0,9 0 3 − 5,9 9 4	3 0,0 0 0 − 4,0 0 0	5 3,3 2 6 − 9 4 7	6 7,3 3 4 − 3,5 5 8

Line up the digits. Then add or subtract.

	a	b
7.	27,002 − 13,849 = _____	62,525 + 13,475 = _____

27,002
−13,849

WORKING WITH WHOLE NUMBERS

Estimation of Sums and Differences

To estimate a sum or difference, first round each number to the same place. Then add or subtract the rounded numbers.

Estimate: 765 + 321

Round each number to the same place. Add.

$$765 \rightarrow 800$$
$$+321 \rightarrow +300$$
$$\overline{1100}$$

Estimate: 2694 − 743

Round each number to the same place. Subtract.

$$2694 \rightarrow 2700$$
$$-743 \rightarrow -700$$
$$\overline{2000}$$

PRACTICE

Estimate the sum.

	a	b	c	d
1.	$248 \rightarrow 200$ $+381 \rightarrow +400$ 600	$264 \rightarrow$ $+375 \rightarrow$	$293 \rightarrow$ $+346 \rightarrow$	$274 \rightarrow$ $+242 \rightarrow$
2.	$638 \rightarrow$ $+291 \rightarrow$	$543 \rightarrow$ $+376 \rightarrow$	$254 \rightarrow$ $+363 \rightarrow$	$181 \rightarrow$ $+475 \rightarrow$
3.	$432 \rightarrow$ $+377 \rightarrow$	$643 \rightarrow$ $+265 \rightarrow$	$375 \rightarrow$ $+430 \rightarrow$	$424 \rightarrow$ $+380 \rightarrow$

Estimate the difference.

	a	b	c	d
4.	$931 \rightarrow 900$ $-779 \rightarrow -800$ 100	$933 \rightarrow$ $-666 \rightarrow$	$622 \rightarrow$ $-159 \rightarrow$	$511 \rightarrow$ $-134 \rightarrow$
5.	$1199 \rightarrow$ $-619 \rightarrow$	$1041 \rightarrow$ $-717 \rightarrow$	$1491 \rightarrow$ $-888 \rightarrow$	$1292 \rightarrow$ $-418 \rightarrow$

PROBLEM SOLVING

Applications

Solve.

1. Apollo 8 flew 550,000 miles on its trip around the moon. Apollo 9 flew 3,700,000 miles on its trip. How many miles were flown by the two spacecraft?

Answer _____

2. In one year 28,762 new books were published. The next year 30,387 books were published. How many books were published during the two years?

Answer _____

3. Cheryl earned $28,529 in her business. During the same period, Percy earned $19,730. Together how much did they earn?

Answer _____

4. On one Saturday, 73,927 people attended a football game. The next week 68,412 people saw the game. How many people saw the two games?

Answer _____

5. The Johnsonville Automobile Club sent out 1736 special books to its members this month. Last month they sent 1402 books. How many more books were sent this month?

Answer _____

6. The Cascade Tunnel in Washington is 41,152 feet long. The Moffat Tunnel in Colorado is 32,798 feet long. How much longer is the Cascade Tunnel than the Moffat Tunnel?

Answer _____

7. The longest tunnel in the world is the Simplon, in the Alps. It is 64,971 feet long. How much longer is it than the bridge in our town which is 1736 feet long?

Answer _____

8. A box of marbles contained 6312 marbles. John added these to his collection. Now he has 14,921 marbles in all. How many marbles did he have before?

Answer _____

WORKING WITH WHOLE NUMBERS
Unit 1 Review

Write the place name for the 4 in each number.

	a		b
1. 3,470,981	_____	3,504,972	_____

Write each number using digits. Insert commas where needed.

2. seventy-two thousand, eighty-five _____

3. two million, forty thousand, five hundred six _____

Compare. Write <, >, or =.

	a		b		c
4. 405	_____ 540	189	_____ 189	368	_____ 2031

Round to the nearest hundred.

	a		b		c
5. 8578	_____	485	_____	1258	_____

Add.

	a	b	c	d
6.	428 +229	167 + 92	64,357 +35,764	27,809 + 2,195

Subtract.

	a	b	c	d
7.	736 −449	1471 − 683	53,647 −28,658	37,853 − 7,865

Line up the digits. Then add.

a	b
8. 449 + 223 + 720 = _____	862 + 687 + 57 = _____

Estimate the sum or difference.

	a	b	c	d
9.	254 → +529 →	244 +398	854 −145	745 −286

MULTIPLICATION

1-digit Numbers

To multiply by 1-digit numbers, use your basic multiplication facts.

Find: 6 × 325

Multiply 5 by 6 ones. Regroup.	Multiply 20 by 6 ones. Regroup.	Multiply 300 by 6 ones.

Th H T O
     3 2 5
×   6
        0
	Th H T O
	   3 2 5
	× 6
	    5 0
		Th H T O
		   3 2 5
		× 6
		 1 9 5 0

PRACTICE

Multiply.

	a	b	c	d	e

1.	H T O
	  3 2
	× 7
	2 2 4
		H T O
		  4 5
		× 3
			H T O
			  8 7
			× 2
				H T O
				  5 6
				× 8
					H T O
					  4 2
					× 7

2.	1 6 8 × 4	6 3 9 × 3	2 6 5 × 7	4 3 1 × 9	5 7 3 × 5
3.	6 7 5 × 2	8 6 × 8	6 6 × 9	2 3 4 × 7	8 1 6 × 4
4.	3 7 × 6	5 6 × 4	2 6 1 × 8	7 2 8 × 3	3 4 1 × 9

Line up the digits. Then multiply.

	a	b	c
5.	83 × 2 = _____ 83 × 2	91 × 5 = _____	211 × 7 = _____
6.	77 × 6 = _____	45 × 8 = _____	957 × 3 = _____

Applications

Solve.

1. Selma has a checking account. She is charged 25¢ for every check she writes. Last month she wrote 3 checks. How much was she charged?

   Answer _____

2. One mile is equal to 1609 meters. How many meters are there in 4 miles?

   Answer _____

3. Esteban has been able to save $250 per year for 7 years. How much did he save in all?

   Answer _____

4. One pound is about 454 grams. How many grams are there in 4 pounds?

   Answer _____

5. Clarence bought 2 pairs of shoes at $22 a pair. How much did he pay for the 2 pairs?

   Answer _____

6. Beth rides 8 miles a day on her bicycle in coming to school and going back home. If she goes to school a total of 175 days in the year, how many miles does she ride?

   Answer _____

7. Jack lives in the country. Each day he rides 38 miles on the bus. How many miles does he ride in 6 days?

   Answer _____

8. Holly sold 4 televisions at $531 each. How much money did she receive?

   Answer _____

MULTIPLICATION
2-digit Numbers by 2-digit Numbers

To multiply, line up the digits. Multiply, starting with the ones digits. Write zeros as placeholders. Add to find the product.

Find: 36 × 46

Multiply by 6 ones. Regroup.	Write a zero. Multiply by 3 tens. Regroup.	Add.
$\begin{array}{r} \overset{3}{4}\,6 \\ \times\ 3\,6 \\ \hline 2\,7\,6 \end{array}$	$\begin{array}{r} \overset{1}{4}\,6 \\ \times\ 3\,6 \\ \hline 2\,7\,6 \\ 1\,3\,8\,0 \end{array}$	$\begin{array}{r} 4\,6 \\ \times\ 3\,6 \\ \hline 2\,7\,6 \\ 1\,3\,8\,0 \\ \hline 1\,6\,5\,6 \end{array}$

GUIDED PRACTICE

Multiply.

	a	*b*	*c*	*d*
1.	$\begin{array}{r} \overset{1}{1}\,4 \\ \times\ 1\,3 \\ \hline 4\,2 \\ 1\,4\,0 \\ \hline 1\,8\,2 \end{array}$	$\begin{array}{r} 4\,1 \\ \times\ 2\,2 \end{array}$	$\begin{array}{r} 2\,7 \\ \times\ 5\,4 \end{array}$	$\begin{array}{r} 3\,2 \\ \times\ 6\,7 \end{array}$
2.	$\begin{array}{r} \overset{4}{2}\,8 \\ \times\ 1\,5 \\ \hline 1\,4\,0 \\ 2\,8\,0 \\ \hline 4\,2\,0 \end{array}$	$\begin{array}{r} 5\,8 \\ \times\ 2\,1 \end{array}$	$\begin{array}{r} 6\,5 \\ \times\ 4\,2 \end{array}$	$\begin{array}{r} 8\,4 \\ \times\ 7\,3 \end{array}$
3.	$\begin{array}{r} 3\,9 \\ \times\ 2\,6 \end{array}$	$\begin{array}{r} 5\,1 \\ \times\ 1\,9 \end{array}$	$\begin{array}{r} 6\,3 \\ \times\ 8\,1 \end{array}$	$\begin{array}{r} 9\,2 \\ \times\ 5\,5 \end{array}$

Multiply.

	a	*b*	*c*	*d*	*e*
1.	5 7 ×3 7	4 8 ×2 5	9 5 ×4 3	6 9 ×1 2	5 3 ×5 6
2.	8 4 ×1 5	7 6 ×9 6	2 3 ×1 2	3 8 ×4 2	8 9 ×1 7
3.	2 4 ×1 8	4 4 ×3 1	3 6 ×2 6	9 9 ×7 7	7 2 ×2 8

Line up the digits. Then multiply.

a	*b*	*c*
4. 52 × 33 = _____	87 × 47 = _____	68 × 61 = _____

33
×52

| **5.** 17 × 28 = _____ | 74 × 34 = _____ | 12 × 49 = _____ |

MIXED PRACTICE

Find each answer.

	a	*b*	*c*	*d*	*e*
1.	3 7 +4 8	7 5 × 6	9 7 −5 2	1 6 × 9	6 7 2 −5 2 7
2.	6 4 3 −3 5 4	8 0 9 +2 6 5	7 8 1 − 9 9	5 9 × 8	8 3 × 4

25

MULTIPLICATION
3-digit Numbers by 2-digit Numbers

To multiply, line up the digits. Multiply, starting with the ones digits. Write zeros as placeholders. Add to find the product.

Find: 69 × 618

Multiply by 9 ones.
Regroup.

TTh	Th	H	T	O
		1	7	
	6	1	8	
×			6	9
	5	5	6	2

Write a zero.
Multiply by 6 tens.
Regroup.

TTh	Th	H	T	O
		1	4	
	6	1	8	
×			6	9
	5	5	6	2
3	7	0	8	0

Add.

TTh	Th	H	T	O
	6	1	8	
×			6	9
	5	5	6	2
3	7	0	8	0
4	2	6	4	2

PRACTICE

Multiply.

	a	b	c	d
1.	741 × 25 3705 14820 18525	912 × 19	158 × 29	226 × 16
2.	345 × 32	128 × 42	512 × 34	414 × 48
3.	659 × 13	783 × 57	595 × 82	297 × 61

Line up the digits. Then multiply.

a

4. 362 × 76 = _____

362
× 76

b

847 × 54 = _____

c

96 × 217 = _____

Zeros in Multiplication

Remember,
- the product of 0 and any number is 0.
- the sum of 0 and any number is that number.

Find: 27 × 608

Multiply by 7 ones. Regroup.	Write a zero. Multiply by 2 tens. Regroup.	Add.

TTh Th H T O
      ⁵
  6 0 8
×   2 7
4 2 5 6
	TTh Th H T O
	      ¹
	  6 0 8
	× 2 7
	4 2 5 6
	1 2 1 6 0
		TTh Th H T O
		  6 0 8
		× 2 7
		  4 2 5 6
		1 2 1 6 0
		1 6 4 1 6

PRACTICE

Multiply.

	a	b	c	d	e
1.	30 × 3 ___ 90	20 × 6	10 × 7	60 × 4	40 × 6
2.	709 × 82	304 × 49	580 × 21	102 × 98	603 × 37
3.	25 ×50 ___ 00 1250 ___ 1250	65 ×10	55 ×70	48 ×20	14 ×30
4.	507 × 20	806 × 40	390 × 60	204 × 90	100 × 20

PROBLEM-SOLVING STRATEGY

Use a Table

You should always look for facts as you read a problem. When many facts are given in a problem, it can be helpful to organize the facts. One way to organize facts is to put them in a table. Then, you can use the table to solve the problem.

Read the problem.

Tony works at a music store. For the past two weeks, all of the records, cassettes, and CDs have been on sale. During the first week of the sale, Tony sold 75 records, 60 cassettes, and 50 CDs. During the second week of the sale, he sold 100 records, 105 cassettes, and 75 CDs. Which was the best-selling item?

List the facts.

Fact 1. Tony sold 75 records, 60 cassettes, and 50 CDs during the first week of the sale.

Fact 2. Tony sold 100 records, 105 cassettes, and 75 CDs during the second week of the sale.

Make a table.

Put in all the facts.

	Records	Cassettes	CDs
First week	75	60	50
Second week	100	105	75
Total			

Solve the problem.

Add the total sales of each item.

$$\begin{array}{r} 75 \\ +100 \\ \hline 175 \text{ records} \end{array} \qquad \begin{array}{r} 60 \\ +105 \\ \hline 165 \text{ cassettes} \end{array} \qquad \begin{array}{r} 50 \\ +75 \\ \hline 125 \text{ CDs} \end{array}$$

The records were the best-selling item.

Read the following problem. Organize the facts in a table. Then, use the table to solve the problems.

The Boy Scouts had a recycling project. They collected 125 pounds of newspaper, 60 pounds of aluminum cans, and 30 pounds of glass during the first week. The next week they collected 198 pounds of newspapers, 75 pounds of aluminum cans, and 42 pounds of glass. During the third week, they collected 198 pounds of newspaper, 80 pounds of aluminum cans, and 68 pounds of glass.

	Newspaper	Cans	Glass
Week 1			
Week 2			
Week 3			

1. How many pounds of newspaper were collected in three weeks?

Answer _____

2. How many pounds of glass were collected in three weeks?

Answer _____

3. How many more pounds of aluminum cans were collected during the second week than the first week?

Answer _____

4. How many pounds of material were collected during the third week?

Answer _____

5. A recycling company pays 50¢ for each pound of aluminum. After 3 weeks, how much money did the Scouts get for their aluminum cans?

Answer _____

6. Another company pays 25¢ for each pound of paper and 10¢ for each pound of glass. How much money did the Scouts collect during the first week for paper and glass?

Answer _____

MULTIPLICATION

Estimation of Products

To estimate products, round each number. Then multiply the rounded numbers.

Estimate: 28 × 44

Round each number to the same place. Multiply.

$$
\begin{array}{r}
44 \rightarrow 40 \\
\times 28 \rightarrow \times 30 \\
\hline
1200
\end{array}
$$

PRACTICE

Estimate.

	a	b	c	d
1.	$\begin{array}{r} 32 \rightarrow 30 \\ \times 57 \rightarrow \times 60 \\ \hline 1800 \end{array}$	$\begin{array}{r} 18 \rightarrow \\ \times 29 \rightarrow \end{array}$	$\begin{array}{r} 46 \rightarrow \\ \times 13 \rightarrow \end{array}$	$\begin{array}{r} 65 \rightarrow \\ \times 21 \rightarrow \end{array}$
2.	$\begin{array}{r} 73 \rightarrow \\ \times 28 \rightarrow \end{array}$	$\begin{array}{r} 84 \rightarrow \\ \times 66 \rightarrow \end{array}$	$\begin{array}{r} 57 \rightarrow \\ \times 39 \rightarrow \end{array}$	$\begin{array}{r} 43 \rightarrow \\ \times 22 \rightarrow \end{array}$
3.	$\begin{array}{r} 92 \rightarrow \\ \times 31 \rightarrow \end{array}$	$\begin{array}{r} 77 \rightarrow \\ \times 37 \rightarrow \end{array}$	$\begin{array}{r} 61 \rightarrow \\ \times 54 \rightarrow \end{array}$	$\begin{array}{r} 88 \rightarrow \\ \times 48 \rightarrow \end{array}$
4.	$\begin{array}{r} 94 \rightarrow \\ \times 35 \rightarrow \end{array}$	$\begin{array}{r} 79 \rightarrow \\ \times 18 \rightarrow \end{array}$	$\begin{array}{r} 52 \rightarrow \\ \times 39 \rightarrow \end{array}$	$\begin{array}{r} 81 \rightarrow \\ \times 24 \rightarrow \end{array}$

Estimate.

	a	b	c
5.	$\begin{array}{r} 27 \times 55 \quad 30 \\ \times 60 \end{array}$	86×12	48×33

PROBLEM SOLVING

Applications

Solve.

1. Rosita took out a loan for a car. She will make 36 payments of $220 each. How much will she pay for the car?

   Answer _____

2. Sam Johnson has a truck that weighs 4725 pounds. The truck will carry a load of 7500 pounds. What is the total weight of truck and full load.

   Answer _____

3. The store has 40 bushels of apples to sell. How many pounds is this if a bushel of apples weighs 58 pounds?

   Answer _____

4. The Martin Real Estate Company bought two houses. One house cost $72,420. The other house cost $89,517. How much did they pay for both?

   Answer _____

5. In an ordinary year there are 365 days. There are 24 hours in a day. How many hours are there in the year?

   Answer _____

6. The first airplane flight to Paris took 26 hours. The average speed was 130 miles an hour. How many miles long was the trip?

   Answer _____

7. The highest point in the continental United States is Mt. Whitney, which is 14,501 feet above sea level. San Antonio, Texas, is 709 feet above sea level. How much difference is there in the heights above sea level of these two places?

   Answer _____

8. Alaska is the largest state in the nation and has an area of 1,518,220 square kilometers. Rhode Island is the smallest state and has an area of 3,231 square kilometers. How many more square kilometers are there in Alaska than in Rhode Island?

   Answer _____

3-digit Numbers by 3-digit Numbers

To multiply, line up the digits. Multiply, starting with the ones digits. Write zeros as placeholders. Add to find the product.

Find: 342 × 576

Multiply by 2 ones. Regroup.	Write a zero. Multiply by 4 tens. Regroup.	Write 2 zeros. Multiply by 3 hundreds. Regroup.	Add.

Th	H	T	O
	1	1	
	5	7	6
×	3	4	2
1	1	5	2

TTh	Th	H	T	O
		3	2	
		5	7	6
×		3	4	2
	1	1	5	2
2	3	0	4	0

HTh	TTh	Th	H	T	O
			2	1	
			5	7	6
×			3	4	2
		1	1	5	2
	2	3	0	4	0
1	7	2	8	0	0

HTh	TTh	Th	H	T	O
			5	7	6
×			3	4	2
		1	1	5	2
	2	3	0	4	0
1	7	2	8	0	0
1	9	6	9	9	2

GUIDED PRACTICE

Multiply.

a

1.

TTh	Th	H	T	O
		4	2	4
×		1	2	2
		8	4	8
	8	4	8	0
4	2	4	0	0
5	1	7	2	8

b

HTh	TTh	Th	H	T	O
			2	5	0
×			4	3	6

c

HTh	TTh	Th	H	T	O
			5	0	9
×			2	6	7

d

HTh	TTh	Th	H	T	O
			7	4	6
×			8	9	1

2.

TTh	Th	H	T	O
		2	3	2
×		2	3	2

HTh	TTh	Th	H	T	O
			5	4	0
×			4	3	2

HTh	TTh	Th	H	T	O
			7	1	4
×			3	6	9

HTh	TTh	Th	H	T	O
			9	1	3
×			5	4	0

Multiply.

	a	b	c	d
1.	3 1 3 ×2 2 3	9 0 7 ×6 4 2	1 7 6 ×3 3 8	6 2 1 ×5 4 8
2.	2 6 2 ×1 7 5	5 1 3 ×2 9 6	7 8 0 ×5 4 3	6 5 2 ×3 7 0
3.	4 6 0 ×1 7 8	5 4 7 ×2 9 0	6 4 5 ×5 3 2	9 7 8 ×1 9 4

Line up the digits. Then multiply.

a	b	c
4. 345 × 273 = _____	487 × 480 = _____	706 × 378 = _____

345
×273

⬠ **MIXED PRACTICE**

Find each answer.

	a	b	c	d
1.	7 3 7 −3 1 6	9 8 9 −3 6 4	8 7 6 +3 4 2	8 8 8 −5 6 5
2.	9 7 8 × 4 3	6 1 5 3 −3 1 3 2	3 9 6 × 7 2	4 7 3 +7 9 7

Choose an Operation

Sometimes a problem does not tell you whether to add, subtract, multiply, or divide. To solve such a problem, you must read the problem carefully. Then, decide what the problem is asking you to do. Next, choose an operation to solve the problem. Finally, solve the problem.

EXAMPLE 1

Read the problem.

Lil saved $60. Gil saved $42. How much money have they saved in all?

Decide what the problem is asking.

In this problem, the question "How much . . . in all?" is asking you to find a sum.

Choose the operation.

To solve, you must add.

Solve the problem.

$60 + $42 = $102
Lil and Gil saved $102 in all.

EXAMPLE 2

Read the problem.

Tim has 5 boxes of books. There are 12 books in each box. How many books does Tim have?

Decide what the problem is asking.

In this problem the question "How many . . ." is asking you to find a total.

Choose the operation.

To solve, you must multiply 12 by 5. Of course you could add 12 five times, but adding would take longer.

Solve the problem.

$12 \times 5 = 60$
Tim has a total of 60 books.

**Choose the correct operation needed to solve each problem.
Then solve the problem.**

1. There are 54 marigold plants, 68 zinnia plants and 49 petunia plants in the greenhouse. How many plants are there in all?

   Operation _____

   Answer _____

2. About 20 bushels of apples came from each tree in the orchard. About how many bushels of apples in all can you get from 7 trees?

   Operation _____

   Answer _____

3. One acre is equal to 4840 square yards. How many square yards are there in 4 acres?

   Operation _____

   Answer _____

4. Jerry rides a bus to work. Each day he rides 16 miles on the bus. How many miles does he ride in 24 days?

   Operation _____

   Answer _____

5. During the first hour there were 17 children at the church nursery. During the second hour, 15 more came. How many children were in the nursery all together after 2 hours?

   Operation _____

   Answer _____

6. Irene had three packages to mail. One weighed 98 grams, the second weighed 130 grams, and the third weighed 210 grams. How much did the packages weigh together?

   Operation _____

   Answer _____

7. Kurt sold 23 papers on Monday, 42 papers on Tuesday, and 37 papers on Wednesday. How many papers did he sell in three days?

   Operation _____

   Answer _____

8. How much will 32 desks cost at $48 each?

   Operation _____

   Answer _____

35

Large Numbers

To multiply large numbers, use the same steps you used to multiply smaller numbers.

Study these examples.

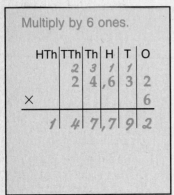

Multiply by 6 ones.	Multiply by 6 ones, 2 tens. Add.	Multiply by 2 ones, 3 tens. Then add.

HTh	TTh	Th	H	T	O
	2	3	1	1	
2	4,	6	3	2	
×					6
1	4	7,	7	9	2

	HTh	TTh	Th	H	T	O
			4	6	7	1
	×				2	6
		2	8	0	2	6 ✔
		9	3	4	2	0
	1	2	1,	4	4	6

M	HTh	TTh	Th	H	T	O
			5	0,	0	0	0
	×					3	2
		1	0	0	0	0 ✔
1	5	0	0	0	0	
1,	6	0	0,	0	0	0

PRACTICE

Multiply.

	a	b	c	d
1.	5 5 3 7 8 9 6 × 6 4 7,3 7 6	4 6 8 7 × 4	2 4 6 8 × 7	5 0 0 0 × 8
2.	2 3,4 5 4 × 2	1 5,0 9 5 × 5	5 4,2 3 3 × 3	7 0,0 0 0 × 9
3.	2 3 9 2 × 5 4	3 0 0 0 × 9 0	5 3,4 0 4 × 1 6	4 2,0 0 0 × 1 9

Line up the digits. Then multiply.

	a	b	c
4.	2 × 4653 = _____	9 × 38,641 = _____	14 × 5207 = _____

4653
× 2

MULTIPLICATION
Unit 2 Review

Multiply.

	a	*b*	*c*	*d*
1.	29 × 5	90 × 6	234 × 2	310 × 7
2.	805 × 8	1511 × 5	7000 × 9	35,672 × 3
3.	64 ×23	59 ×34	45 ×17	311 × 92
4.	235 × 26	241 × 48	2605 × 64	4000 × 30
5.	2005 × 87	11,847 × 42	20,709 × 37	16,321 × 51
6.	700 ×200	830 ×463	378 ×195	567 ×308

---

7. How much did Sharon pay for 2 pounds of nuts at 46¢ per pound?

8. If potatoes weigh 60 pounds to the bushel, how much do 245 bushels weigh?

Answer _____

Answer _____

To divide by a 1-digit divisor, first decide on a trial quotient. Then multiply and subtract.

Remember, if your trial quotient is too large or too small, try another number.

Find: 378 ÷ 6

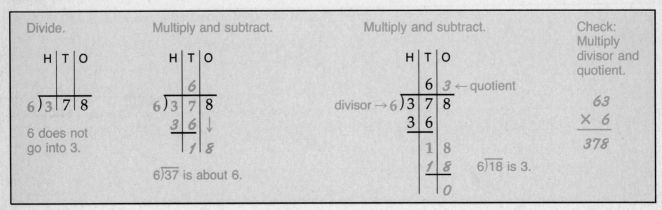

PRACTICE

Divide.

	a	b	c	d	e

1.

a
```
  T O
  1 2
8)9 6
  8 ↓
  1 6
  1 6
    0
```

b
```
T O
4)7 6
```

c
```
T O
3)8 1
```

d
```
H T O
2)9 4 6
```

e
```
H T O
8)9 6 8
```

2.

```
2)1 9 6      6)3 3 6      7)1 5 4      9)8 3 7      3)4 2 3
```

Set up the problem. Then divide.

a
3. 96 ÷ 6 = _____

```
6)96
```

b
435 ÷ 5 = _____

c
891 ÷ 9 = _____

PROBLEM SOLVING

Applications

Solve.

1. In 5 months Hector saved $305. He saved the same amount each month. How much did he save each month?

   Answer _____

2. Walter drove his car 207 miles on 9 gallons of gas. How many miles did he get to the gallon?

   Answer _____

3. In a bicycle race Jane rode her bicycle 126 kilometers in 3 hours. How many kilometers did she average for the 3 hours?

   Answer _____

4. Jenny scored 132 points in 6 basketball games. How many points did she score on the average per game?

   Answer _____

5. James is packaging books. There are 4 books in a box. How many boxes will he need for 228 books?

   Answer _____

6. How many nickels are there in 65 cents? Remember that a nickel is 5 cents.

   Answer _____

7. On a trip last week George drove 392 miles in 8 hours. How many miles per hour did he average?

   Answer _____

8. In an hour 7 people delivered 455 telephone directories. How many directories did each person average for this delivery?

   Answer _____

9. There are 3 feet in a yard. How many yards of fencing are needed to enclose a park that measures 651 feet?

   Answer _____

10. Maria bought 2 blouses for the same price. She spent $36. How much did each blouse cost?

   Answer _____

DIVISION
1-digit Divisors with Remainders

To divide, first decide on a trial quotient. If your trial quotient is too large or too small, try another number. Multiply and subtract. Write the remainder in the quotient.

Find: 749 ÷ 5

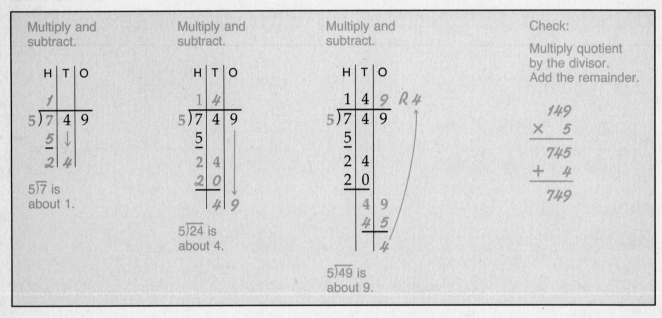

GUIDED PRACTICE

Divide.

	a	b	c	d

1.

a. T O — 6)6 7 with quotient 11 R 1

b. T O — 3)4 4

c. T O — 5)7 6

d. T O — 7)8 8

2.

a. T O — 8)1 0 with quotient 1 R 2

b. H T O — 4)1 3 9

c. Th H T O — 8)6 9 1 1

d. Th H T O — 7)1 0 1 3

40

Divide.

a	b	c	d
1. 6)5 9	5)6 8	3)8 5	8)2 6 6
2. 4)3 4 7	2)1 1 7	7)3 0 0	9)5 5 7
3. 5)7 4 8	8)9 5 8	3)8 9 0	6)7 1 9
4. 2)8 4 3	9)1 9 1 2	4)1 4 4 7	7)2 6 2 3

Set up the problem. Then divide.

       a   b   c

5. $37 \div 2 =$ _____ $41 \div 3 =$ _____ $214 \div 9 =$ _____

6. $345 \div 6 =$ _____ $627 \div 5 =$ _____ $188 \div 8 =$ _____

MIXED PRACTICE

Find each answer.

a	b	c	d
1. 1 5 9 9 +8 2 9 4	8 5 × 7	2 0 6 − 2 5	1 7 2 9 −1 2 3 7

Make a Drawing

When you read a problem, you might not know at once how to solve it. When that happens, a drawing may help you solve the problem. You should always read the problem carefully and look for facts. Next, make a drawing to help you keep track of the facts. Then, solve the problem.

Read the problem.

> Jimmy makes deliveries for the grocery store. One day, he started from the store and walked 3 blocks north to make his first delivery. Then Jimmy walked 2 blocks east for the second delivery. His third delivery was 5 blocks south of his second delivery. Jimmy's final delivery was 2 blocks west of his third. How far does Jimmy have to walk to get back to the store?

List the facts.

> Fact 1. Jimmy started from the grocery store.
> Fact 2. Jimmy walked 3 blocks north.
> Fact 3. Then, Jimmy walked 2 blocks east.
> Fact 4. Next, he walked 5 blocks south.
> Fact 5. Finally, Jimmy walked 2 blocks west.

Make a drawing.

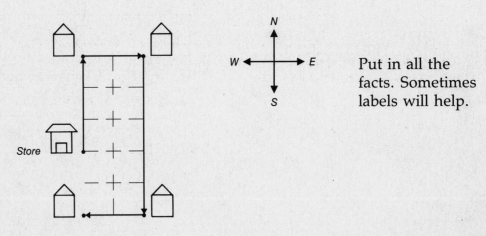

Put in all the facts. Sometimes labels will help.

Solve the problem.

> From the drawing you can see that Jimmy has to walk 2 blocks to get back to the store.

For each of the following problems, make a drawing or diagram.
Put in all the facts and then solve the problem.

1. A field is in the shape of a rectangle. Its length is 30 feet. Its width is 10 feet. How many feet of wire are needed to go around that field?

Answer _____

2. Velma drove 150 miles from her house toward Washington, D.C. A few hours later, Wilma left Velma's house and drove 70 miles in the same direction. How far apart were Velma and Wilma then?

Answer _____

3. Lou lives 40 miles east of Centerville. His friend Myra lives 50 miles west of Centerville. How far do Lou and Myra live from one another?

Answer _____

4. A museum has a special drawer for rock samples. The drawer holds 4 rows of 5 boxes each. Each box holds 2 rocks. How many rocks fit into the drawer?

Answer _____

Zeros in Quotients

To divide, decide on a trial quotient. Then multiply and subtract.
Remember to divide every time you bring down a number.

Find: 325 ÷ 3

Multiply and subtract.

```
    H T O
    1
3 ) 3 2 5      3)3 is 1.
    3 ↓
      2
```

Multiply and subtract.

```
    H T O
    1 0↙
3 ) 3 2 5      3 does not
    3          go into 2.
    2          Write a
    0 ↓        zero in the
    2 5        quotient.
```

Multiply and subtract.

```
    H T O
    1 0 8 R1
3 ) 3 2 5      3)25 is about 8.
    3
    2
    0
    2 5
    2 4
        1
```

PRACTICE

Divide.

	a	b	c	d
1.	1 0 9 R 4 5) 5 4 9 5 ↓ 4 0 ↓ 4 9 4 5 4	2) 8 1 5	7) 7 3 8	3) 9 2 3
2.	5 0 ↙ 3) 1 5 0 1 5 0	5) 2 0 2	9) 7 2 3 4	8) 4 8 3 2

DIVISION

2-digit Divisors: Multiples of 10

To divide, decide on a trial quotient. Then multiply and subtract.

Find: 760 ÷ 60

Multiply and subtract.	Multiply and subtract.	Check:

Multiply and subtract.

$$\begin{array}{r} 1 \\ 60\overline{)760} \\ 60\downarrow \\ \hline 160 \end{array}$$

Think: $6\overline{)7}$ is about 1.
So, $60\overline{)76}$
Put the 1 above the 6.

Multiply and subtract.

$$\begin{array}{r} 1\,2 \text{ R } 40 \\ 60\overline{)760} \\ 60 \\ \hline 160 \\ 120 \\ \hline 40 \end{array}$$

Think: $6\overline{)16}$ is about 2.
So, $60\overline{)160}$

Check:

$$\begin{array}{r} 12 \\ \times\ 60 \\ \hline 720 \\ +\ 40 \\ \hline 760 \end{array}$$

PRACTICE

Divide.

	a	b	c	d
1.	$\begin{array}{r}18\text{ R }37\\50\overline{)937}\\50\downarrow\\\hline437\\400\\\hline37\end{array}$	$30\overline{)978}$	$20\overline{)860}$	$40\overline{)885}$
2.	$\begin{array}{r}13\\80\overline{)1040}\\80\\\hline240\\240\\\hline0\end{array}$	$70\overline{)2620}$	$60\overline{)1560}$	$90\overline{)4430}$

Set up the problem. Then divide.

	a	b	c
3.	1285 ÷ 20 = _____	1670 ÷ 60 = _____	3760 ÷ 80 = _____

$20\overline{)1285}$

Applications

Solve.

1. A bus company charters buses to groups. Each bus will hold 62 passengers. How many people can travel on 9 buses?

Answer _____

2. Gracie wants to buy a car that costs $12,340. An air conditioner will cost $625 more. How much will the car with an air conditioner cost?

Answer _____

3. A truck loaded with coal weighed a total of 9200 pounds. After the coal was unloaded the truck weighed 3275 pounds. How many pounds of coal were unloaded?

Answer _____

4. The Declaration of Independence was signed in 1776. How many years ago was that? (Use the present year.)

Answer _____

5. A plane flew at an altitude of 20,732 feet on its first flight. On a later flight it flew at an altitude of 32,684 feet. What was the altitude difference in the two flights?

Answer _____

6. To build a terrace, Leona bought 3 truckloads of crushed rock. Each load weighed 2304 pounds. How much did all of the rock weigh?

Answer _____

7. On a trip Matthew counted 283 cars. Arturo counted 197 cars. How many cars were counted by Matthew and Arturo?

Answer _____

8. The Bicycle Safety Council had 7000 leaflets to distribute in two months. In September 4690 leaflets were given out. How many leaflets were left to be distributed in October?

Answer _____

9. Six people bought a tent costing $96. Each person paid the same amount. What was each person's share of the price of the tent?

Answer _____

10. Texas gained its independence in 1836. How long ago was that? (Use the present year.)

Answer _____

Trial Quotients: Too Large or Too Small

When you divide, your trial quotient may be too large or too small. Decide on a trial quotient, multiply and subtract. Check your trial quotient. If your trial quotient is too large or too small, try again.

Find: 928 ÷ 32

Decide on a trial quotient.	Multiply and subtract.	Try a smaller number. Multiply and subtract.	Finish the problem.
$32\overline{)928}$	$\begin{array}{r} 3 \\ 32\overline{)928} \\ 96 \end{array}$	$\begin{array}{r} 2 \\ 32\overline{)928} \\ 64 \\ \hline 28 \end{array}$	$\begin{array}{r} 29 \\ 32\overline{)928} \\ 64\downarrow \\ \hline 288 \\ 288 \\ \hline 0 \end{array}$
Think: 3$\overline{)9}$ is about 3. So, 32$\overline{)92}$ is about 3.	Since 96 > 92, 3 is too large.	Since 28 < 32, 2 is correct.	

Find: 896 ÷ 28

$28\overline{)896}$	$\begin{array}{r} 2 \\ 28\overline{)896} \\ 56 \\ \hline 33 \end{array}$	$\begin{array}{r} 3 \\ 28\overline{)896} \\ 84 \\ \hline 5 \end{array}$	$\begin{array}{r} 32 \\ 28\overline{)896} \\ 84\downarrow \\ \hline 56 \\ 56 \\ \hline 0 \end{array}$
28 rounds to 30. Think: 3$\overline{)8}$ is about 2. So, 28$\overline{)89}$ is about 2.	Since 33 > 28, 2 is too small.	Since 5 < 28, 3 is correct.	

PRACTICE

Identify the given trial quotient as too large or too small. Write the correct trial quotient on the line.

            a   *b*

1. $\begin{array}{r} 4 \\ 22\overline{)858} \\ 88 \end{array}$ _4 is too large._   3 $\begin{array}{r} 2 \\ 26\overline{)795} \end{array}$ _____

2. $\begin{array}{r} 3 \\ 31\overline{)907} \end{array}$ _____ $\begin{array}{r} 7 \\ 51\overline{)3542} \end{array}$ _____

3. $\begin{array}{r} 7 \\ 45\overline{)3688} \end{array}$ _____ $\begin{array}{r} 5 \\ 87\overline{)4241} \end{array}$ _____

DIVISION
2-digit Divisors

To divide by a 2-digit divisor, decide on a trial quotient. Multiply and subtract. Write the remainder in the quotient.

Find: 569 ÷ 43

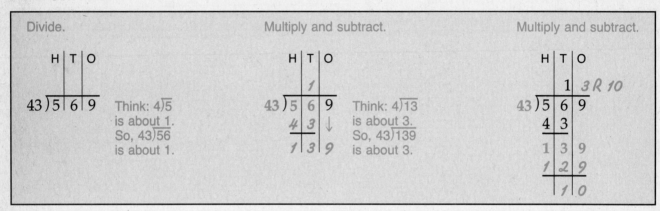

Divide.	Multiply and subtract.	Multiply and subtract.

Divide.

```
  H T O
      1
43)5 6 9      Think: 4)5
              is about 1.
              So, 43)56
              is about 1.
```

Multiply and subtract.

```
  H T O
      1
43)5 6 9      Think: 4)13
  4 3  ↓      is about 3.
  1 3 9       So, 43)139
              is about 3.
```

Multiply and subtract.

```
  H T O
      1 3 R 10
43)5 6 9
  4 3
  1 3 9
  1 2 9
    1 0
```

GUIDED PRACTICE

Divide.

           a   *b*   *c*

1.

```
  H T O
    1 4 R 27
45)6 5 7
  4 5 ↓
  2 0 7
  1 8 0
    2 7
```

```
  H T O
38)8 3 6
```

```
  H T O
61)9 5 4
```

2.

```
  H T O
      9 R 60
75)7 3 5
  6 7 5
    6 0
```

```
  H T O
52)1 2 6
```

```
  H T O
91)3 8 2
```

3.

```
TTh Th H T O
 36)1 1 6 6 9
```

```
TTh Th H T O
 53)2 2 1 6 1
```

```
TTh Th H T O
 17)1 1 4 8 3
```

PRACTICE

Divide.

	a	b	c	d
1.	$\begin{array}{r} 7R4 \\ 12\overline{)88} \\ \underline{84} \\ 4 \end{array}$	$13\overline{)65}$	$16\overline{)96}$	$17\overline{)54}$
2.	$15\overline{)465}$	$32\overline{)672}$	$41\overline{)839}$	$24\overline{)944}$
3.	$82\overline{)1312}$	$43\overline{)2200}$	$26\overline{)1898}$	$17\overline{)5176}$
4.	$55\overline{)17270}$	$38\overline{)19927}$	$74\overline{)30313}$	$63\overline{)10584}$

Set up the problem. Then divide.

	a	b	c
5.	$38 \div 12 =$ _____	$882 \div 42 =$ _____	$931 \div 71 =$ _____
	$12\overline{)38}$		

 MIXED PRACTICE

Find each answer.

	a	b	c	d
1.	$6\overline{)2634}$	$\begin{array}{r} 79 \\ \times 62 \end{array}$	$30\overline{)7143}$	$\begin{array}{r} 208 \\ \times\ 82 \end{array}$

49

PROBLEM-SOLVING STRATEGY

Choose an Operation

Sometimes a problem does not tell you whether to add, subtract, multiply, or divide. To solve such a problem, you must read the problem carefully. Then, decide what the problem is asking you to do. Next, choose an operation to solve the problem. Finally, solve the problem.

EXAMPLE 1

Read the problem.

The museum has 354 rare stones in its collection. If 225 of these stones are placed on display, how many rare stones are left and are not on display?

Decide what the problem is asking.

In this problem, the question "how many . . . are left" is asking you to find a difference.

Choose the operation.

To solve, you must subtract.

Solve the problem.

$354 - 225 = 129$
The museum has 129 rare stones not on display.

EXAMPLE 2

Read the problem.

A passenger train of 12 cars is carrying 720 passengers. If each car carries the same number of passengers, how many passengers are in each car?

Decide what the problem is asking.

In this problem, the question "how many . . . in each" is asking you to find an average, or equal parts.

Choose the operation.

To solve, you must divide.

Solve the problem.

$720 \div 12 = 60$
There are 60 passengers in each car.

Choose the correct operation needed to solve each problem. Then solve the problem.

1. Last year Mrs. Sanchez earned $17,534. This year she will earn $18,760. How much more will she earn this year?

   Operation _____

   Answer _____

2. On a car trip we drove 728 miles in 14 hours. How many miles per hour did we average?

   Operation _____

   Answer _____

3. A merchant paid $252 for 36 shirts. How much is this for each shirt?

   Operation _____

   Answer _____

4. Mary Beth traveled 880 miles in 16 hours. What was her average rate of speed?

   Operation _____

   Answer _____

5. A bridge on the Pennsylvania Railroad is 3850 feet in length. How much less than a mile is this? (5280 feet in a mile)

   Operation _____

   Answer _____

6. Ms. Thomas is a bricklayer. Yesterday she worked 11 hours and earned $132. How much is this per hour?

   Operation _____

   Answer _____

7. How much heavier was the elephant Jumbo, who weighed 13,660 pounds, than Queenie, who weighed 11,987 pounds?

   Operation _____

   Answer _____

8. The total weight of 35 boxes of freight is 2695 pounds. What is the average weight of each box?

   Operation _____

   Answer _____

DIVISION

Estimating Quotients

To estimate quotients, use rounded numbers.

Estimate: 345 ÷ 5

Round to use a basic fact.	Think:	Divide.
$5\overline{)3\,4\,5}$	$5 \times 7 = 35$	$\dfrac{70}{5\overline{)350}}$

Estimate: 828 ÷ 23

Round each number.	Divide.
$828 \rightarrow 800$ $23 \rightarrow 20$	$\dfrac{40}{20\overline{)800}}$

PRACTICE

Estimate using basic facts.

	a	b	c
1.	$3\overline{)2\,7\,2} \rightarrow 3\overline{)270}^{\,90}$	$7\overline{)4\,1\,9} \rightarrow$	$9\overline{)3\,6\,3} \rightarrow$
2.	$5\overline{)4\,1\,8} \rightarrow 5\overline{)400}^{\,80}$	$3\overline{)1\,6\,7} \rightarrow$	$6\overline{)2\,3\,3} \rightarrow$

Estimate by rounding both numbers.

	a	b	c
3.	$3\,6\overline{)7\,5\,6} \rightarrow 40\overline{)800}^{\,20}$	$2\,8\overline{)9\,2\,4} \rightarrow$	$1\,7\overline{)5\,7\,8} \rightarrow$
4.	$5\,2\overline{)9\,8\,8} \rightarrow$	$3\,1\overline{)8\,9\,9} \rightarrow$	$4\,3\overline{)7\,7\,4} \rightarrow$

DIVISION

Unit 3 Review

Divide.

	a	*b*	*c*	*d*
1.	$4\overline{)92}$	$8\overline{)600}$	$5\overline{)295}$	$9\overline{)108}$
2.	$3\overline{)50}$	$6\overline{)561}$	$7\overline{)425}$	$2\overline{)1014}$
3.	$20\overline{)840}$	$30\overline{)1050}$	$70\overline{)63000}$	$80\overline{)16108}$
4.	$38\overline{)988}$	$64\overline{)1344}$	$42\overline{)1600}$	$57\overline{)3673}$
5.	$83\overline{)18509}$	$23\overline{)14287}$	$36\overline{)14527}$	$51\overline{)21624}$

Solve.

6. If each bus carries 44 people, how many buses will be needed to carry 352 people to the picnic?

7. Judy's car can travel 315 miles on 15 gallons of gasoline. How many miles per gallon does her car get?

Answer _____

Answer _____

Meaning of Fractions

A fraction names *part* of a whole. This circle has 3 equal parts. Each part is $\frac{1}{3}$ of the circle.

2 of the 3 equal parts are shaded blue.

numerator
2—two blue parts
3—three parts in all
denominator

We read $\frac{2}{3}$ as two thirds.

A fraction also names *part* of a group. Three of the five triangles are shaded blue.

3—three blue triangles
5—five triangles in all

Three fifths are blue.

GUIDED PRACTICE

Write the fraction and the word name for the part that is shaded.

a	b	c

1.

$\frac{1}{5}$ _____ or ___one fifth___   _____ or _____   _____ or _____

2.

_____ or _____   _____ or _____   _____ or _____

Write the fraction for the word name.

a   b   c

3. two sevenths __$\frac{2}{7}$__   three fourths _____   six ninths _____

Write the word name for the fraction.

a   b   c

4. $\frac{5}{8}$ ___five eighths___ $\frac{4}{7}$ _____ $\frac{1}{4}$ _____

Write the fraction and the word name for the part that is shaded.

	a	*b*	*c*

1.

_____ or _____   _____ or _____   _____ or _____

Write the fraction for the word name.

a	*b*	*c*
2. nine tenths _____	six sixths _____	two eighths _____
3. five sevenths _____	ten twelfths _____	four ninths _____

Write the word name for the fraction.

a	*b*	*c*
4. $\frac{1}{3}$ _____	$\frac{7}{9}$ _____	$\frac{5}{5}$ _____
5. $\frac{6}{7}$ _____	$\frac{3}{10}$ _____	$\frac{9}{12}$ _____

There are 7 days in a week. Each day is $\frac{1}{7}$ week. Write the following as a fraction of a week. Write the word name for the fraction.

a	*b*	*c*
6. 4 days = $\frac{4}{7}$ week	5 days = _____ week	2 days = _____ week
four sevenths		

There are 20 nickels in a dollar. Each nickel is $\frac{1}{20}$ dollar. Write the following as a fraction of a dollar. Write the word name for the fraction.

a	*b*	*c*
7. 6 nickels = $\frac{6}{20}$ dollar	11 nickels = _____ dollar	8 nickels = _____ dollar
six twentieths		

MIXED PRACTICE

Line up the digits. Then find each answer.

a	*b*	*c*
1. 15 + 39 = _____	52 − 28 = _____	120 − 87 = _____
2. 81 × 18 = _____	355 ÷ 15 = _____	71 × 117 = _____

Equivalent Fractions

Equivalent fractions name the same number. Compare the circles. The shaded part of one circle is equal to the shaded part of the other circle. What part of each circle is shaded?

$\frac{1}{2}$ of the circle is shaded. $\frac{3}{6}$ of the circle is shaded.

$\frac{1}{2}$ and $\frac{3}{6}$ are equivalent fractions. $\frac{1}{2} = \frac{3}{6}$

PRACTICE

The figure at the right is divided into 8 equal parts.

Each part is $\frac{1}{8}$ of the figure.

Write the equivalent fractions.

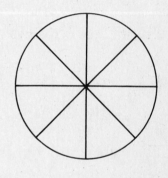

1. How many $\frac{1}{8}$ parts are in $\frac{1}{4}$ of the figure? _____ *2* $\frac{1}{4} = \frac{2}{8}$

2. How many $\frac{1}{8}$ parts are in $\frac{1}{2}$ of the figure? _____ $\frac{1}{2} = \frac{}{8}$

3. How many $\frac{1}{8}$ parts are in $\frac{3}{4}$ of the figure? _____ $\frac{3}{4} = \frac{}{8}$

4. How many $\frac{1}{8}$ parts are in $\frac{2}{4}$ of the figure? _____ $\frac{2}{4} = \frac{}{8}$

Write two equivalent fractions for the shaded part of each figure.

a   b

5.

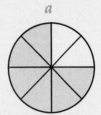   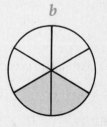

$\frac{3}{4} = \frac{6}{8}$

_____   _____

6.

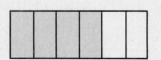   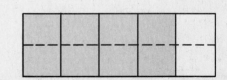

_____   _____

Comparing and Ordering Fractions

Number lines can be used to compare and order fractions. On a number line, the fractions become greater as you move from the left to the right.

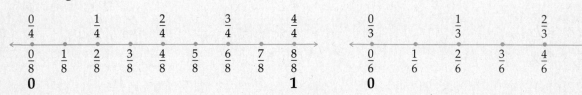
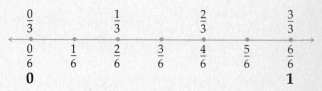

Compare $\frac{1}{8}$ and $\frac{3}{8}$.

Find $\frac{1}{8}$ and $\frac{3}{8}$ on the number line. Since $\frac{1}{8}$ is farther to the left, it is less than $\frac{3}{8}$.

$$\frac{1}{8} < \frac{3}{8}$$

Compare $\frac{4}{4}$ and $\frac{8}{8}$.

Find $\frac{4}{4}$ and $\frac{8}{8}$ on the number line. They name the same mark on the line.

$$\frac{4}{4} = \frac{8}{8} = 1$$

Compare $\frac{2}{3}$ and $\frac{2}{6}$.

Find $\frac{2}{3}$ and $\frac{2}{6}$ on the number line. Since $\frac{2}{3}$ is farther to the right, it is greater than $\frac{2}{6}$.

$$\frac{2}{3} > \frac{2}{6}$$

PRACTICE

Use the number lines above to compare these fractions. Write <, >, or =.

	a		*b*		*c*		*d*
1.	$\frac{7}{8}$ > $\frac{2}{8}$		$\frac{3}{3}$ ___ $\frac{6}{6}$		$\frac{3}{6}$ ___ $\frac{5}{6}$		$\frac{1}{3}$ ___ $\frac{2}{6}$
2.	$\frac{5}{8}$ ___ $\frac{8}{8}$		$\frac{3}{6}$ ___ $\frac{1}{6}$		$\frac{3}{3}$ ___ $\frac{1}{3}$		$\frac{4}{8}$ ___ $\frac{5}{8}$
3.	$\frac{1}{4}$ ___ $\frac{2}{4}$		$\frac{1}{4}$ ___ $\frac{2}{8}$		$\frac{5}{8}$ ___ $\frac{7}{8}$		$\frac{1}{6}$ ___ $\frac{2}{3}$
4.	$\frac{4}{6}$ ___ $\frac{2}{3}$		$\frac{3}{3}$ ___ $\frac{5}{6}$		$\frac{4}{8}$ ___ $\frac{2}{4}$		$\frac{3}{8}$ ___ $\frac{3}{4}$

Write the fractions in order from least to greatest.

	a		*b*
5.	$\frac{7}{8}$ $\frac{3}{4}$ $\frac{3}{8}$ ___ $\frac{3}{8}$ $\frac{3}{4}$ $\frac{7}{8}$		$\frac{1}{3}$ $\frac{3}{6}$ $\frac{1}{6}$ ___
6.	$\frac{2}{3}$ $\frac{2}{6}$ $\frac{5}{6}$ ___		$\frac{1}{4}$ $\frac{2}{4}$ $\frac{3}{8}$ ___
7.	$\frac{3}{8}$ $\frac{1}{8}$ $\frac{3}{4}$ ___		$\frac{2}{3}$ $\frac{1}{3}$ $\frac{3}{6}$ ___
8.	$\frac{6}{6}$ $\frac{2}{3}$ $\frac{1}{6}$ ___		$\frac{7}{8}$ $\frac{1}{4}$ $\frac{4}{8}$ ___

Equivalent Fractions in Higher Terms

To add or subtract fractions, you might need to change a fraction to an equivalent form. To change a fraction to an equivalent fraction in higher terms, multiply the numerator and the denominator by the same nonzero number.

Rewrite $\frac{1}{2}$ with 6 as the denominator.

Compare the denominators.

$\frac{1}{2} = \frac{}{6}$ Think: $2 \times 3 = 6$.

Multiply the numerator and the denominator by 3.

$\frac{1}{2} = \frac{1 \times 3}{2 \times 3} = \frac{3}{6}$

PRACTICE

Multiply to rewrite each fraction as an equivalent fraction in higher terms.

	a	b	c
1.	$\frac{1}{3} = \frac{1 \times 4}{3 \times 4} = \frac{4}{12}$	$\frac{2}{5} = \frac{2 \times}{5 \times} = \frac{}{15}$	$\frac{3}{4} = \frac{3 \times}{4 \times} = \frac{}{16}$
2.	$\frac{3}{8} = \frac{3 \times}{8 \times} = \frac{}{16}$	$\frac{2}{3} = \frac{2 \times}{3 \times} = \frac{}{9}$	$\frac{1}{2} = \frac{1 \times}{2 \times} = \frac{}{16}$
3.	$\frac{3}{4} = \frac{3 \times}{4 \times} = \frac{}{12}$	$\frac{5}{8} = \frac{5 \times}{8 \times} = \frac{}{16}$	$\frac{2}{9} = \frac{2 \times}{9 \times} = \frac{}{18}$
4.	$\frac{2}{3} = \frac{2 \times}{3 \times} = \frac{}{12}$	$\frac{2}{5} = \frac{2 \times}{5 \times} = \frac{}{10}$	$\frac{3}{5} = \frac{3 \times}{5 \times} = \frac{}{25}$

Rewrite each fraction as an equivalent fraction in higher terms.

	a	b	c	d
5.	$\frac{4}{5} = \frac{8}{10}$	$\frac{1}{4} = \frac{}{12}$	$\frac{7}{8} = \frac{}{16}$	$\frac{1}{5} = \frac{}{20}$
6.	$\frac{1}{3} = \frac{}{15}$	$\frac{5}{6} = \frac{}{12}$	$\frac{3}{5} = \frac{}{15}$	$\frac{4}{5} = \frac{}{15}$
7.	$\frac{1}{2} = \frac{}{12}$	$\frac{3}{4} = \frac{}{20}$	$\frac{3}{10} = \frac{}{20}$	$\frac{7}{9} = \frac{}{18}$
8.	$\frac{1}{5} = \frac{}{25}$	$\frac{2}{3} = \frac{}{15}$	$\frac{1}{2} = \frac{}{8}$	$\frac{4}{7} = \frac{}{14}$
9.	$\frac{1}{2} = \frac{}{10}$	$\frac{5}{9} = \frac{}{18}$	$\frac{2}{7} = \frac{}{14}$	$\frac{1}{3} = \frac{}{9}$
10.	$\frac{4}{9} = \frac{}{18}$	$\frac{3}{8} = \frac{}{16}$	$\frac{5}{6} = \frac{}{18}$	$\frac{1}{4} = \frac{}{20}$

Equivalent Fractions in Simplest Terms

Sometimes you might need to change a fraction to an equivalent fraction in simplest terms. To change a fraction to an equivalent fraction in simplest terms, divide the numerator and the denominator by the greatest number possible.

Write $\frac{6}{8}$ in simplest terms.

Consider the numerator and denominator.

$\frac{6}{8} =$ Think: 8 can be divided evenly by 4 but 6 cannot.
6 can be divided evenly by 3 but 8 cannot.
Both 8 and 6 can be divided evenly by 2.

Divide the numerator and the denominator by 2.

$$\frac{6}{8} = \frac{6 \div 2}{8 \div 2} = \frac{3}{4}$$

A fraction is in simplest terms when 1 is the greatest number that divides the numerator and the denominator. The fraction $\frac{3}{4}$ is in simplest terms.

PRACTICE

Divide to write each fraction as an equivalent fraction in simplest terms.

	a	b	c
1.	$\frac{5}{15} = \frac{5 \div 5}{15 \div 5} = \frac{1}{3}$	$\frac{8}{10} = \frac{8 \div}{10 \div} =$	$\frac{9}{12} = \frac{9 \div}{12 \div} =$
2.	$\frac{4}{6} = \frac{4 \div}{6 \div} =$	$\frac{14}{16} = \frac{14 \div}{16 \div} =$	$\frac{10}{25} = \frac{10 \div}{25 \div} =$
3.	$\frac{2}{8} = \frac{2 \div}{8 \div} =$	$\frac{4}{8} = \frac{4 \div}{8 \div} =$	$\frac{3}{9} = \frac{3 \div}{9 \div} =$
4.	$\frac{8}{16} = \frac{8 \div}{16 \div} =$	$\frac{2}{16} = \frac{2 \div}{16 \div} =$	$\frac{2}{4} = \frac{2 \div}{4 \div} =$

Write each fraction as an equivalent fraction in simplest terms.

	a	b	c	d
5.	$\frac{12}{16} = \frac{3}{4}$	$\frac{2}{6} =$ ___	$\frac{4}{12} =$ ___	$\frac{8}{12} =$ ___
6.	$\frac{4}{16} =$ ___	$\frac{6}{10} =$ ___	$\frac{6}{9} =$ ___	$\frac{2}{10} =$ ___
7.	$\frac{2}{12} =$ ___	$\frac{3}{15} =$ ___	$\frac{6}{12} =$ ___	$\frac{10}{15} =$ ___
8.	$\frac{8}{14} =$ ___	$\frac{5}{25} =$ ___	$\frac{10}{18} =$ ___	$\frac{6}{8} =$ ___
9.	$\frac{15}{18} =$ ___	$\frac{3}{12} =$ ___	$\frac{4}{14} =$ ___	$\frac{20}{25} =$ ___
10.	$\frac{5}{10} =$ ___	$\frac{8}{18} =$ ___	$\frac{4}{10} =$ ___	$\frac{6}{16} =$ ___

Improper Fractions and Mixed Numbers

An improper fraction is a fraction with a numerator that is greater than or equal to the denominator.

$\frac{4}{4}$, $\frac{12}{4}$ and $\frac{7}{4}$ are improper fractions.

An improper fraction can be written as a whole or mixed number.

A mixed number is a whole number and a fraction.

$2\frac{1}{3}$ is a mixed number.

A mixed number can be written as an improper fraction.

Write $\frac{4}{4}$ and $\frac{12}{4}$ as whole numbers.

Divide the numerator by denominator.

$4\overline{)4}$ $\frac{4}{4} = 1$

$4\overline{)12}$ $\frac{12}{4} = 3$

Write $\frac{7}{4}$ as a mixed number.

Divide the numerator by the denominator. Write the remainder as a fraction by writing the remainder over the divisor.

$4\overline{)7}$ $\frac{7}{4} = 1\frac{3}{4}$

Write $2\frac{1}{3}$ as an improper fraction.

Multiply the whole number and the denominator. Add this product to the numerator. Then write the sum over the denominator.

$$2\frac{1}{3} = \frac{2 \times 3 + 1}{3} = \frac{6 + 1}{3} = \frac{7}{3}$$

$$2\frac{1}{3} = \frac{7}{3}$$

GUIDED PRACTICE

Write as a whole number.

	a	b	c	d
1.	$\frac{20}{5} = \underline{4}$	$\frac{16}{8} = \underline{2}$	$\frac{60}{10} = \underline{6}$	$\frac{84}{12} = \underline{7}$
2.	$\frac{63}{9} = \underline{7}$	$\frac{18}{6} = \underline{3}$	$\frac{56}{4} = \underline{14}$	$\frac{14}{14} = \underline{1}$

Write as a mixed number.

	a	b	c	d
3.	$\frac{13}{12} = \underline{1\frac{1}{12}}$	$\frac{18}{7} = \underline{\quad}$	$\frac{13}{4} = \underline{\quad}$	$\frac{17}{5} = \underline{\quad}$
4.	$\frac{15}{8} = \underline{\quad}$	$\frac{12}{11} = \underline{\quad}$	$\frac{16}{9} = \underline{\quad}$	$\frac{8}{3} = \underline{\quad}$

Write as an improper fraction.

	a	b	c	d
5.	$1\frac{4}{5} = \underline{\frac{9}{5}}$	$4\frac{3}{7} = \underline{\quad}$	$1\frac{1}{9} = \underline{\quad}$	$3\frac{3}{4} = \underline{\quad}$
6.	$5\frac{1}{4} = \underline{\quad}$	$2\frac{2}{5} = \underline{\quad}$	$3\frac{3}{8} = \underline{\quad}$	$1\frac{5}{8} = \underline{\quad}$

PRACTICE

Write as a mixed number or whole number.

	a	b	c	d
1.	$\frac{6}{5} =$ _____	$\frac{5}{3} =$ _____	$\frac{32}{6} =$ _____	$\frac{18}{12} =$ _____
2.	$\frac{12}{5} =$ _____	$\frac{16}{3} =$ _____	$\frac{12}{9} =$ _____	$\frac{19}{4} =$ _____
3.	$\frac{21}{12} =$ _____	$\frac{23}{6} =$ _____	$\frac{13}{2} =$ _____	$\frac{20}{8} =$ _____
4.	$\frac{36}{9} =$ _____	$\frac{12}{12} =$ _____	$\frac{16}{8} =$ _____	$\frac{54}{6} =$ _____

Write as an improper fraction.

	a	b	c	d
5.	$4\frac{1}{4} =$ _____	$3\frac{2}{3} =$ _____	$4\frac{1}{2} =$ _____	$1\frac{1}{6} =$ _____
6.	$2\frac{1}{4} =$ _____	$1\frac{7}{8} =$ _____	$4\frac{1}{3} =$ _____	$3\frac{4}{5} =$ _____
7.	$4\frac{2}{3} =$ _____	$1\frac{1}{10} =$ _____	$2\frac{3}{5} =$ _____	$2\frac{5}{7} =$ _____
8.	$2\frac{2}{9} =$ _____	$4\frac{2}{5} =$ _____	$5\frac{1}{2} =$ _____	$4\frac{1}{6} =$ _____

 MIXED PRACTICE

Add or subtract.

	a	b	c	d
1.	729 76 + 15	722 273 + 68	871 − 87	981 +653
2.	29 136 +5326	15,970 −10,955	2090 − 387	503 −230
3.	29,076 +10,135	7360 +4041	13,053 + 8,120	6893 −1239

Addition and Subtraction of Fractions with Like Denominators

To add or subtract fractions with like denominators, add or subtract the numerators. Use the same denominator. Simplify the answer.

Remember,
- to simplify an improper fraction, write it as a whole number or mixed number.
- to simplify a proper fraction, write it in simplest terms.

Find: $\frac{3}{5} + \frac{4}{5}$

Add the numerators.	Use the same denominator.
$\frac{3}{5}$	$\frac{3}{5}$
$+\frac{4}{5}$	$+\frac{4}{5}$
$\frac{7}{}$	$\frac{7}{5} = 1\frac{2}{5}$
	Simplify the answer.

Find: $\frac{7}{8} - \frac{3}{8}$

Subtract the numerators.	Use the same denominator.
$\frac{7}{8}$	$\frac{7}{8}$
$-\frac{3}{8}$	$-\frac{3}{8}$
$\frac{4}{}$	$\frac{4}{8} = \frac{1}{2}$
	Simplify the answer.

GUIDED PRACTICE

Add. Simplify.

	a	b	c	d	e
1.	$\frac{5}{12}$ $+\frac{3}{12}$ $\frac{8}{12} = \frac{2}{3}$	$\frac{4}{9}$ $+\frac{2}{9}$	$\frac{3}{7}$ $+\frac{1}{7}$	$\frac{3}{8}$ $+\frac{1}{8}$	$\frac{4}{9}$ $+\frac{3}{9}$
2.	$\frac{3}{5}$ $+\frac{3}{5}$ $\frac{6}{5} = 1\frac{1}{5}$	$\frac{4}{5}$ $+\frac{3}{5}$	$\frac{3}{8}$ $+\frac{6}{8}$	$\frac{2}{3}$ $+\frac{2}{3}$	$\frac{7}{8}$ $+\frac{1}{8}$

Subtract. Simplify.

	a	b	c	d	e
3.	$\frac{5}{8}$ $-\frac{1}{8}$ $\frac{4}{8} = \frac{1}{2}$	$\frac{6}{6}$ $-\frac{4}{6}$	$\frac{5}{8}$ $-\frac{3}{8}$	$\frac{5}{6}$ $-\frac{2}{6}$	$\frac{5}{9}$ $-\frac{2}{9}$

PRACTICE

Add or subtract. Simplify.

	a	*b*	*c*	*d*	*e*	*f*
1.	$\frac{1}{4}$ $+\frac{2}{4}$	$\frac{2}{6}$ $+\frac{3}{6}$	$\frac{3}{8}$ $+\frac{2}{8}$	$\frac{1}{9}$ $+\frac{3}{9}$	$\frac{1}{8}$ $+\frac{4}{8}$	$\frac{1}{6}$ $+\frac{4}{6}$
2.	$\frac{7}{8}$ $-\frac{3}{8}$	$\frac{9}{16}$ $-\frac{5}{16}$	$\frac{3}{4}$ $-\frac{1}{4}$	$\frac{5}{6}$ $-\frac{3}{6}$	$\frac{7}{9}$ $-\frac{4}{9}$	$\frac{8}{9}$ $-\frac{2}{9}$
3.	$\frac{3}{6}$ $+\frac{2}{6}$	$\frac{5}{9}$ $+\frac{2}{9}$	$\frac{9}{12}$ $-\frac{5}{12}$	$\frac{12}{15}$ $-\frac{3}{15}$	$\frac{12}{20}$ $-\frac{8}{20}$	$\frac{5}{8}$ $+\frac{1}{8}$
4.	$\frac{3}{5}$ $-\frac{1}{5}$	$\frac{7}{10}$ $-\frac{5}{10}$	$\frac{9}{10}$ $-\frac{7}{10}$	$\frac{7}{8}$ $-\frac{1}{8}$	$\frac{5}{6}$ $-\frac{1}{6}$	$\frac{7}{10}$ $-\frac{2}{10}$

Add or subtract. Simplify.

         a   *b*   *c*

5. $\frac{2}{4} + \frac{1}{4} =$ _____ $\frac{7}{8} - \frac{5}{8} =$ _____ $\frac{7}{8} - \frac{3}{8} =$ _____

MIXED PRACTICE

Round each number to the nearest hundred.

	a	*b*	*c*	*d*	*e*
1.	85 _____	170 _____	251 _____	1029 _____	23,448 _____

Estimate the product.

	a	*b*	*c*	*d*
2.	3 5 0 $\times$ 4	6 8 1 $\times$ 2 9	8 8 $\times$2 2	3 1 8 $\times$ 9

Find a Pattern

The answer to a problem may be found by recognizing a pattern.
Read the problem carefully. Write the pattern and determine how
the numbers are related. Find the rule that makes and completes
the pattern. Then solve the problem.

EXAMPLE 1

Read the problem.

What are the next two numbers in this number pattern? 1, 4, 16, . . .

Determine the relationship.

$$\overset{\times 4}{\frown}\ \overset{\times 4}{\frown}$$
$$1 \quad 4 \quad 16 \ldots$$

Write the rule.

Multiply by 4.

Solve the problem.

$16 \times 4 = 64 \qquad 64 \times 4 = 256$
The next two numbers are 64 and 256.

EXAMPLE 2

Read the problem.

In a volleyball tournament each team plays another team only once.
If there are two teams, 1 game would be played. Three teams would
play 3 games. Four teams would play 6 games. How many games
would be played by five teams?

Write the pattern.

The number pattern was not given to you. A table will help you
write the pattern.

Teams	2	3	4	5
Games	1	3	6	?

Determine the relationship.

$$\overset{+2}{\frown}\ \overset{+3}{\frown}$$
$$1 \quad 3 \quad 6 \ldots$$

Write the rule.

Add 2; add 3; add 4 and so on.

Solve the problem.

$6 + 4 = 10$
Five teams would play 10 games.

64

Solve by finding the pattern. Write the rule. Then answer the question.

1. What is the next number in the pattern?
2, 6, 18, . . .

Rule _____

Answer _____

2. What are the next two numbers in this pattern?
25, 20, 15, . . .

Rule _____

Answer _____

3. What is the next number in this pattern?
112, 56, 28, . . .

Rule _____

Answer _____

4. What is the missing number in this pattern?
15, 30, _____, 60

Rule _____

Answer _____

Write the number pattern. Then answer the question.

5. The first five multiples of 11 are 11, 22, 33, 44, 55. Write the number pattern for the sum of the digits in each multiple. What would the next number be in this pattern?

Pattern _____

Answer _____

6. A square can be made with 4 toothpicks. It takes 7 toothpicks to make two squares side by side. Three squares in a row can be made with 10 toothpicks. How many toothpicks would you need to make four squares in a row?

Pattern _____

Answer _____

7. The Fibonacci sequence is a number pattern that starts with two ones. The first six numbers are 1, 1, 2, 3, 5, 8. Find the next two numbers in this sequence. (Each number is the sum of the two numbers before it.)

Pattern _____

Answer _____

8. The first four multiples of 12 are 12, 24, 36, 48. Write the number pattern for the sum of the digits in each multiple. What would the next number be in this pattern?

Pattern _____

Answer _____

Applications

Solve.

1. Ruby lives $\frac{1}{2}$ mile from work. Adele lives $\frac{1}{2}$ mile beyond Ruby. How far from work does Adele live?

Answer _____

2. Jack lived $\frac{1}{4}$ mile west of the store. Jill lived $\frac{3}{4}$ mile east of the store. How far was it from Jack's to Jill's?

Answer _____

3. Janice Davis used $\frac{3}{8}$ pound of nuts for muffins and $\frac{5}{8}$ pound of nuts for banana bread. How many pounds of nuts in all did she use?

Answer _____

4. Joe's recipe uses $\frac{3}{4}$ cup of white flour and $\frac{3}{4}$ cup of whole-wheat flour. How much flour will he use in all?

Answer _____

5. Miguel bought 12 ounces of tea. What fractional part of a pound did he buy? (1 pound = 16 ounces)

Answer _____

6. Sofia has a half-dollar and a quarter. What fractional part of a dollar does she have in all?

Answer _____

7. Bill went to visit some of his friends and walked $\frac{1}{4}$ mile, $\frac{3}{4}$ mile, $\frac{1}{4}$ mile, and $\frac{3}{4}$ mile. How far did he walk altogether?

Answer _____

8. What fractional part of a dollar is each of the following coins? (1 dollar = 100 cents)

10¢ =   50¢ =

25¢ =   5¢ =

Addition and Subtraction of Mixed Numbers with Like Denominators

To add or subtract mixed numbers with like denominators, first add or subtract the fractions. Then add or subtract the whole numbers and simplify.

Find: $1\frac{1}{8} + 2\frac{5}{8}$

Add the fractions.	Add the whole numbers. Simplify.
$\begin{array}{r} 1\frac{1}{8} \\ +2\frac{5}{8} \\ \hline \frac{6}{8} \end{array}$	$\begin{array}{r} 1\frac{1}{8} \\ +2\frac{5}{8} \\ \hline 3\frac{6}{8} = 3\frac{3}{4} \end{array}$

Find: $8\frac{5}{9} - 4\frac{2}{9}$

Subtract the fractions.	Subtract the whole numbers. Simplify.
$\begin{array}{r} 8\frac{5}{9} \\ -4\frac{2}{9} \\ \hline \frac{3}{9} \end{array}$	$\begin{array}{r} 8\frac{5}{9} \\ -4\frac{2}{9} \\ \hline 4\frac{3}{9} = 4\frac{1}{3} \end{array}$

PRACTICE

Add. Simplify.

	a	b	c	d	e
1.	$\begin{array}{r} 2\frac{1}{4} \\ +3\frac{1}{4} \\ \hline 5\frac{2}{4} = 5\frac{1}{2} \end{array}$	$\begin{array}{r} 3\frac{2}{4} \\ +6\frac{1}{4} \\ \hline \end{array}$	$\begin{array}{r} 9\frac{3}{5} \\ +5\frac{1}{5} \\ \hline \end{array}$	$\begin{array}{r} 7\frac{1}{8} \\ +2\frac{3}{8} \\ \hline \end{array}$	$\begin{array}{r} 4\frac{3}{10} \\ +5\frac{3}{10} \\ \hline \end{array}$
2.	$\begin{array}{r} 8\frac{1}{5} \\ +9\frac{3}{5} \\ \hline \end{array}$	$\begin{array}{r} 6\frac{1}{4} \\ +9\frac{2}{4} \\ \hline \end{array}$	$\begin{array}{r} 6\frac{1}{3} \\ +5\frac{1}{3} \\ \hline \end{array}$	$\begin{array}{r} 12\frac{2}{5} \\ +9\frac{1}{5} \\ \hline \end{array}$	$\begin{array}{r} 12\frac{2}{9} \\ +4\frac{4}{9} \\ \hline \end{array}$

Subtract. Simplify.

	a	b	c	d	e
3.	$\begin{array}{r} 4\frac{11}{12} \\ -2\frac{1}{12} \\ \hline 2\frac{10}{12} = 2\frac{5}{6} \end{array}$	$\begin{array}{r} 3\frac{7}{8} \\ -2\frac{3}{8} \\ \hline \end{array}$	$\begin{array}{r} 6\frac{7}{12} \\ -2\frac{5}{12} \\ \hline \end{array}$	$\begin{array}{r} 5\frac{9}{10} \\ -3\frac{7}{10} \\ \hline \end{array}$	$\begin{array}{r} 7\frac{5}{6} \\ -2\frac{1}{6} \\ \hline \end{array}$
4.	$\begin{array}{r} 7\frac{5}{8} \\ -4\frac{3}{8} \\ \hline \end{array}$	$\begin{array}{r} 6\frac{3}{8} \\ -1\frac{1}{8} \\ \hline \end{array}$	$\begin{array}{r} 8\frac{4}{5} \\ -3\frac{2}{5} \\ \hline \end{array}$	$\begin{array}{r} 5\frac{5}{12} \\ -4\frac{1}{12} \\ \hline \end{array}$	$\begin{array}{r} 8\frac{7}{10} \\ -4\frac{3}{10} \\ \hline \end{array}$

Addition of Fractions with Different Denominators

To add fractions with different denominators, first rewrite the fractions as equivalent fractions with like denominators. Then add and simplify the answer.

Find: $\frac{1}{3} + \frac{5}{6}$

Write equivalent fractions with like denominators.	Add the numerators. Use the same denominator.
$\frac{1}{3} = \frac{2}{6}$ Remember: $\quad$ $+\frac{5}{6} = \frac{5}{6}$ $\quad$ $\frac{1}{3} = \frac{1 \times 2}{3 \times 2} = \frac{2}{6}$	$\frac{1}{3} = \frac{2}{6}$ $\quad$ $+\frac{5}{6} = \frac{5}{6}$ $\quad$ $\frac{7}{6} = 1\frac{1}{6}$ Simplify the answer.

GUIDED PRACTICE

Add. Simplify.

       a   *b*   *c*   *d*

1. $\frac{1}{6} = \frac{1}{6}$ $\frac{3}{10} = \frac{}{10}$ $\frac{1}{8} = \frac{}{8}$ $\frac{1}{2} = \frac{}{6}$

    $+\frac{1}{3} = \frac{2}{6}$ $+\frac{1}{2} = \frac{}{10}$ $+\frac{3}{4} = \frac{}{8}$ $+\frac{1}{6} = \frac{}{6}$

       $\frac{3}{6} = \frac{1}{2}$

2. $\frac{3}{5} = \frac{6}{10}$ $\frac{6}{7} = \frac{}{14}$ $\frac{8}{9} = \frac{}{9}$ $\frac{10}{12} = \frac{}{12}$

    $+\frac{7}{10} = \frac{7}{10}$ $+\frac{5}{14} = \frac{}{14}$ $+\frac{2}{3} = \frac{}{9}$ $+\frac{3}{4} = \frac{}{12}$

       $\frac{13}{10} = 1\frac{3}{10}$

3. $\frac{5}{12} = \frac{}{12}$ $\frac{3}{8} = \frac{}{8}$ $\frac{1}{2} = \frac{}{16}$ $\frac{1}{3} = \frac{}{9}$

    $+\frac{2}{3} = \frac{}{12}$ $+\frac{3}{4} = \frac{}{8}$ $+\frac{8}{16} = \frac{}{16}$ $+\frac{7}{9} = \frac{}{9}$

Add. Simplify.

	a	*b*	*c*	*d*

1.
$$\frac{1}{8} = \frac{1}{8}$$
$$+\frac{1}{4} = \frac{2}{8}$$
$$\frac{3}{8}$$

$$\frac{1}{5}$$
$$+\frac{3}{10}$$

$$\frac{3}{10}$$
$$+\frac{1}{2}$$

$$\frac{3}{4}$$
$$+\frac{1}{8}$$

2.
$$\frac{9}{10} = \frac{9}{10}$$
$$+\frac{1}{5} = \frac{2}{10}$$
$$\frac{11}{10} = 1\frac{1}{10}$$

$$\frac{7}{12}$$
$$+\frac{1}{3}$$

$$\frac{2}{3}$$
$$+\frac{4}{9}$$

$$\frac{7}{12}$$
$$+\frac{5}{6}$$

3.
$$\frac{7}{8}$$
$$+\frac{1}{2}$$

$$\frac{2}{3}$$
$$+\frac{8}{9}$$

$$\frac{3}{4}$$
$$+\frac{3}{8}$$

$$\frac{4}{5}$$
$$+\frac{9}{10}$$

4.
$$\frac{7}{12}$$
$$+\frac{1}{4}$$

$$\frac{2}{3}$$
$$+\frac{5}{9}$$

$$\frac{1}{3}$$
$$+\frac{2}{9}$$

$$\frac{7}{10}$$
$$+\frac{2}{5}$$

Add. Simplify.

	a	*b*	*c*

5. $\frac{2}{3} + \frac{5}{12} = $ _____

$$\frac{2}{3}$$
$$+\frac{5}{12}$$

$\frac{3}{16} + \frac{5}{8} = $ _____

$\frac{3}{4} + \frac{3}{16} = $ _____

6. $\frac{3}{4} + \frac{7}{8} = $ _____

$\frac{6}{7} + \frac{5}{14} = $ _____

$\frac{1}{2} + \frac{7}{8} = $ _____

 MIXED PRACTICE

Line up the digits. Then add or subtract.

	a	*b*	*c*

1. $2019 - 1258 = $ _____ $857 - 485 = $ _____ $732 + 585 = $ _____

Subtraction of Fractions with Different Denominators

To subtract fractions with different denominators, first rewrite the fractions as equivalent fractions with like denominators. Then subtract and simplify the answer.

Find: $\frac{9}{10} - \frac{1}{2}$

Write equivalent fractions with like denominators.

$$\frac{9}{10} = \frac{9}{10}$$
$$-\frac{1}{2} = \frac{5}{10}$$

Remember:
$$\frac{1}{2} = \frac{1 \times 5}{2 \times 5} = \frac{5}{10}$$

Subtract the numerators. Use the same denominator.

$$\frac{9}{10} = \frac{9}{10}$$
$$-\frac{1}{2} = \frac{5}{10}$$
$$\frac{4}{10} = \frac{2}{5} \quad \text{Simplify the answer.}$$

GUIDED PRACTICE

Subtract. Simplify.

	a	*b*	*c*	*d*
1.	$\frac{1}{2} = \frac{4}{8}$ $-\frac{1}{8} = \frac{1}{8}$ $\frac{3}{8}$	$\frac{1}{3} = \frac{}{6}$ $-\frac{1}{6} = \frac{}{6}$	$\frac{3}{4} = \frac{}{4}$ $-\frac{1}{2} = \frac{}{4}$	$\frac{5}{6} = \frac{}{6}$ $-\frac{2}{3} = \frac{}{6}$
2.	$\frac{13}{14} = \frac{13}{14}$ $-\frac{3}{7} = \frac{6}{14}$ $\frac{7}{14} = \frac{1}{2}$	$\frac{1}{2} = \frac{}{6}$ $-\frac{1}{6} = \frac{}{6}$	$\frac{4}{5} = \frac{}{10}$ $-\frac{3}{10} = \frac{}{10}$	$\frac{7}{20} = \frac{}{20}$ $-\frac{1}{4} = \frac{}{20}$
3.	$\frac{4}{5} = \frac{}{10}$ $-\frac{1}{10} = \frac{}{10}$	$\frac{13}{15} = \frac{}{15}$ $-\frac{1}{5} = \frac{}{15}$	$\frac{3}{4} = \frac{}{16}$ $-\frac{1}{16} = \frac{}{16}$	$\frac{11}{12} = \frac{}{12}$ $-\frac{1}{6} = \frac{}{12}$

Subtract. Simplify.

	a	*b*	*c*	*d*

1. $\dfrac{7}{8} = \dfrac{7}{8}$
$-\dfrac{3}{4} = \dfrac{6}{8}$
$\dfrac{1}{8}$

$\dfrac{7}{10}$
$-\dfrac{3}{5}$

$\dfrac{3}{4}$
$-\dfrac{3}{8}$

$\dfrac{3}{8}$
$-\dfrac{1}{4}$

2. $\dfrac{2}{3} = \dfrac{4}{6}$
$-\dfrac{1}{6} = \dfrac{1}{6}$
$\dfrac{3}{6} = \dfrac{1}{2}$

$\dfrac{5}{6}$
$-\dfrac{1}{2}$

$\dfrac{7}{10}$
$-\dfrac{1}{2}$

$\dfrac{9}{16}$
$-\dfrac{1}{4}$

3. $\dfrac{7}{9}$
$-\dfrac{2}{3}$

$\dfrac{13}{16}$
$-\dfrac{1}{4}$

$\dfrac{8}{9}$
$-\dfrac{1}{3}$

$\dfrac{7}{10}$
$-\dfrac{2}{5}$

Subtract. Simplify.

	a	*b*	*c*

4. $\dfrac{17}{20} - \dfrac{1}{2} =$ _____

$\dfrac{13}{15} - \dfrac{1}{3} =$ _____

$\dfrac{11}{16} - \dfrac{1}{2} =$ _____

$\dfrac{17}{20}$
$-\dfrac{1}{2}$

5. $\dfrac{11}{15} - \dfrac{2}{3} =$ _____

$\dfrac{11}{12} - \dfrac{5}{6} =$ _____

$\dfrac{3}{4} - \dfrac{1}{12} =$ _____

 MIXED PRACTICE

Find each answer.

	a	*b*	*c*	*d*

1.
   $\begin{array}{r} 226 \\ 720 \\ +1227 \\ \hline \end{array}$

   $\begin{array}{r} 20,910 \\ -\ \ 1,443 \\ \hline \end{array}$

   $\begin{array}{r} 449 \\ \times\ \ 23 \\ \hline \end{array}$

   $\begin{array}{r} 239 \\ 87 \\ 451 \\ +876 \\ \hline \end{array}$

2.
   $\begin{array}{r} 809 \\ \times\ \ 58 \\ \hline \end{array}$

   $50\overline{)713}$

   $23\overline{)40{,}652}$

   $\begin{array}{r} 45,060 \\ -34,679 \\ \hline \end{array}$

71

PROBLEM-SOLVING STRATEGY

Work Backwards

When you are given an end result, you need to work backwards to solve the problem. First read the problem carefully to find helpful clues. Once you have found the clues, you can work backwards to solve the problem.

Read the problem.

> Ted has 25 model cars. Lucia has 30 model cars. Last week, Ted traded 5 model cars to Lucia for 2 of her cars. How many cars did Lucia have before the trade?

List the clues.

> Clue 1. Lucia has 30 model cars.
> Clue 2. Ted gave 5 cars to Lucia.
> Clue 3. Lucia gave 2 cars to Ted.

Solve the problem.

30	Lucia has 30 cars now.
− 5	Lucia received 5 cars from Ted. Subtract out 5 cars.
25	

$$\downarrow$$

25	
+ 2	Lucia gave 2 cars to Ted. Add back 2 cars.
27	

Before the trade, Lucia had 27 cars.

Work backwards to solve the following problems.

1. George took some money to the fair. He spent $5 on game tickets, and $2 on lunch. He had $3 left. How much money did George take to the fair?

Answer _____

2. Jan spent $15 for two new shirts and $20 for a pair of jeans. She has $5 left. How much money did Jan take shopping?

Answer _____

3. A farmer planted 86 acres of soybeans and 65 acres of corn. Last year, 20 of the acres now used for corn were used for soybeans. How many acres of corn did the farmer have last year?

Answer _____

4. A club treasury ended the week with $76. On Friday, the treasurer had received $35 in club dues. On Tuesday, she had paid a bill of $15. How much money was in the treasury at the beginning of the week?

Answer _____

5. Wong has a herd of sheep. He bought more sheep and this doubled the original number of sheep. He was given 6 more sheep. If Wong now has 46 sheep, how many did he start with?

Answer _____

6. I am thinking of a number. If you divide that number by 2 and subtract 4, the result is 39. What number am I thinking of?

Answer _____

Applications

Solve.

1. Tom lived $\frac{7}{8}$ mile from Cindie, and Tim lived $\frac{3}{8}$ mile beyond Tom. How far from Cindie did Tim live?

Answer _____

2. Esther needs $1\frac{3}{4}$ yards of lace for trimming a dress and $\frac{3}{4}$ yard for a handkerchief. How many yards does she need all together?

Answer _____

3. Richard had $1\frac{1}{2}$ dozen eggs in a large bowl. James brought home $2\frac{1}{2}$ dozen more. How many did they have all together?

Answer _____

4. Ruth wants to build two shelves. One is to be $3\frac{1}{3}$ feet long and the other is to be $4\frac{2}{3}$ feet long. How long a board does she need for both shelves?

Answer _____

5. On an auto trip last summer we went $\frac{2}{9}$ of the way the first day and $\frac{5}{9}$ the second day. What part of the trip did we cover in the first two days?

Answer _____

6. Brad weighs $122\frac{1}{2}$ pounds and Marita weighs $109\frac{1}{2}$ pounds. How much do they weigh together?

Answer _____

7. Delores caught one fish weighing $12\frac{3}{4}$ pounds and another fish weighing $11\frac{3}{4}$ pounds. How much did the two fish together weigh?

Answer _____

8. A storekeeper has sold $2\frac{1}{2}$ yards of material from a bolt of cloth that had contained $6\frac{1}{2}$ yards. How many yards of the material are left?

Answer _____

Unit 4 Review

Write each fraction as an equivalent fraction in simplest terms.

	a	*b*	*c*	*d*
1.	$\frac{9}{12} =$ _____	$\frac{6}{10} =$ _____	$\frac{4}{6} =$ _____	$\frac{4}{8} =$ _____

Rewrite each fraction as an equivalent fraction in higher terms.

	a	*b*	*c*	*d*
2.	$\frac{2}{3} = \frac{}{9}$	$\frac{1}{6} = \frac{}{12}$	$\frac{3}{5} = \frac{}{15}$	$\frac{1}{2} = \frac{}{10}$

Write as a mixed number or whole number.

	a	*b*	*c*	*d*
3.	$\frac{31}{8} =$ _____	$\frac{13}{6} =$ _____	$\frac{25}{5} =$ _____	$\frac{19}{4} =$ _____

Write as an improper fraction.

	a	*b*	*c*	*d*
4.	$4\frac{1}{3} =$ _____	$8\frac{2}{5} =$ _____	$2\frac{1}{8} =$ _____	$5\frac{3}{10} =$ _____
5.	$1\frac{2}{4} =$ _____	$5\frac{6}{8} =$ _____	$4\frac{3}{9} =$ _____	$8\frac{10}{15} =$ _____

Add or subtract. Simplify.

	a	*b*	*c*	*d*
6.	$\frac{1}{8}$ $+\frac{4}{8}$	$\frac{3}{10}$ $+\frac{3}{10}$	$\frac{11}{12}$ $-\frac{7}{12}$	$\frac{5}{6}$ $-\frac{2}{6}$
7.	$2\frac{1}{3}$ $+5\frac{1}{3}$	$6\frac{2}{9}$ $+3\frac{4}{9}$	$8\frac{9}{10}$ $-4\frac{3}{10}$	$9\frac{7}{8}$ $-1\frac{1}{8}$
8.	$\frac{3}{8}$ $+\frac{1}{4}$	$\frac{1}{3}$ $+\frac{7}{9}$	$\frac{11}{16}$ $-\frac{3}{8}$	$\frac{14}{15}$ $-\frac{1}{3}$
9.	$\frac{7}{8}$ $-\frac{1}{2}$	$\frac{1}{2}$ $+\frac{1}{16}$	$\frac{2}{3}$ $-\frac{1}{9}$	$\frac{3}{5}$ $+\frac{3}{10}$

Addition of Mixed Numbers with Different Denominators

To add mixed numbers with different denominators, write the mixed numbers with like denominators. Add the fractions. Then add the whole numbers and simplify.

Find: $3\frac{5}{12} + 5\frac{1}{3}$

Write the mixed numbers with like denominators.	Add the fractions.	Add the whole numbers.	Simplify.
$3\frac{5}{12} = 3\frac{5}{12}$ $+5\frac{1}{3} = 5\frac{4}{12}$ Remember: $5\frac{1}{3} = 5\frac{4}{12}$ and they are equivalent fractions.	$3\frac{5}{12} = 3\frac{5}{12}$ $+5\frac{1}{3} = 5\frac{4}{12}$ $\frac{9}{12}$	$3\frac{5}{12} = 3\frac{5}{12}$ $+5\frac{1}{3} = 5\frac{4}{12}$ $8\frac{9}{12}$	$8\frac{9}{12} = 8\frac{3}{4}$

GUIDED PRACTICE

Add. Simplify.

	a	b	c	d
1.	$3\frac{1}{8} = 3\frac{1}{8}$ $+6\frac{3}{4} = 6\frac{6}{8}$ $9\frac{7}{8}$	$9\frac{2}{3} = 9\frac{\ }{6}$ $+1\frac{1}{6} = 1\frac{1}{6}$	$4\frac{1}{2} = 4\frac{\ }{12}$ $+1\frac{5}{12} = 1\frac{5}{12}$	$2\frac{5}{8} = 2\frac{5}{8}$ $+6\frac{1}{4} = 6\frac{\ }{8}$
2.	$7\frac{1}{3} = 7\frac{5}{15}$ $+2\frac{1}{15} = 2\frac{1}{15}$ $9\frac{6}{15} = 9\frac{2}{5}$	$11\frac{1}{3} =$ $+\ 3\frac{1}{6} =$	$6\frac{3}{4} =$ $+7\frac{1}{12} =$	$2\frac{1}{4} =$ $+5\frac{7}{12} =$
3.	$12\frac{3}{4} =$ $+\ 4\frac{1}{8} =$	$5\frac{3}{8} =$ $+15\frac{1}{2} =$	$8\frac{2}{3} =$ $+3\frac{1}{9} =$	$7\frac{1}{10} =$ $+6\frac{3}{5} =$
4.	$5\frac{5}{8} =$ $+4\frac{1}{4} =$	$15\frac{5}{12} =$ $+\ 8\frac{1}{3} =$	$6\frac{3}{10} =$ $+10\frac{1}{5} =$	$9\frac{2}{3} =$ $+8\frac{2}{9} =$

PRACTICE

Add. Simplify.

	a	*b*	*c*	*d*
1.	$1\frac{1}{10} = 1\frac{1}{10}$ $+9\frac{1}{2} = 9\frac{5}{10}$ $\overline{\quad 10\frac{6}{10} = 10\frac{3}{5}}$	$2\frac{3}{10}$ $+8\frac{2}{5}$	$5\frac{1}{8}$ $+4\frac{3}{4}$	$5\frac{1}{5}$ $+9\frac{3}{10}$
2.	$2\frac{1}{3}$ $+5\frac{7}{12}$	$2\frac{1}{8}$ $+3\frac{1}{2}$	$9\frac{3}{5}$ $+6\frac{1}{15}$	$7\frac{7}{8}$ $+20\frac{1}{16}$
3.	$12\frac{3}{20}$ $+27\frac{1}{4}$	$2\frac{3}{4}$ $+26\frac{1}{8}$	$4\frac{7}{15}$ $+49\frac{1}{3}$	$5\frac{5}{12}$ $+18\frac{1}{4}$
4.	$6\frac{7}{10}$ $+31\frac{1}{5}$	$26\frac{1}{5}$ $+\ 7\frac{7}{15}$	$19\frac{3}{8}$ $+18\frac{5}{16}$	$13\frac{5}{8}$ $+29\frac{1}{4}$

Line up the digits. Add and simplify.

	a	*b*	*c*
5.	$5\frac{5}{12} + 7\frac{1}{3} = $ _____ $5\frac{5}{12}$ $+7\frac{1}{3}$	$12\frac{4}{9} + 19\frac{1}{3} = $ _____	$6\frac{2}{15} + 18\frac{1}{5} = $ _____
6.	$3\frac{3}{10} + 16\frac{1}{2} = $ _____	$14\frac{1}{10} + 24\frac{3}{20} = $ _____	$7\frac{3}{5} + 18\frac{2}{15} = $ _____

 MIXED PRACTICE

Add or subtract.

	a	*b*	*c*	*d*
1.	4 5 6 6 + 5 2 4	3 9 5 5 − 2 3 6 3	7 3 7 3 + 5 4 1 7	9 1,2 0 7 − 8 5,6 0 2

77

Addition of Mixed Numbers with Regrouping

When adding mixed numbers, sometimes your sum will contain an improper fraction. To regroup a sum that contains an improper fraction, first write the improper fraction as a mixed number. Then add and simplify.

Find: $6\frac{2}{3} + 2\frac{5}{6}$

Write the fractions with like denominators. Add the mixed numbers.	The sum, $8\frac{9}{6}$, contains an improper fraction. To regroup, write the improper fraction as a mixed number.	Then add the whole numbers.
$\begin{aligned} 6\frac{2}{3} &= 6\frac{4}{6} \\ +2\frac{5}{6} &= 2\frac{5}{6} \\ \hline &\;\; 8\frac{9}{6} \end{aligned}$	$\frac{9}{6} = 1\frac{3}{6}$	$8\frac{9}{6} = 8 + 1\frac{3}{6} = 9\frac{3}{6}$ Simplify. $9\frac{3}{6} = 9\frac{1}{2}$

GUIDED PRACTICE

Regroup. Simplify.

	a	*b*	*c*	*d*
1.	$3\frac{5}{3}$ $\frac{5}{3} = 1\frac{2}{3}$ $3 + 1\frac{2}{3} = 4\frac{2}{3}$	$6\frac{13}{10}$	$9\frac{9}{8}$	$12\frac{7}{4}$
2.	$4\frac{8}{6}$	$8\frac{12}{9}$	$7\frac{18}{12}$	$10\frac{14}{8}$

Add. Regroup. Simplify.

	a	*b*	*c*
3.	$\begin{aligned} 2\frac{3}{4} &= 2\frac{3}{4} \\ +1\frac{1}{2} &= 1\frac{2}{4} \\ \hline 3\frac{5}{4} &= 3 + 1\frac{1}{4} = 4\frac{1}{4} \end{aligned}$	$\begin{aligned} 4\frac{5}{8} &= \\ +2\frac{3}{4} &= \\ \hline \end{aligned}$	$\begin{aligned} 5\frac{9}{10} &= \\ +3\frac{2}{5} &= \\ \hline \end{aligned}$
4.	$\begin{aligned} 4\frac{2}{3} &= 4\frac{8}{12} \\ +8\frac{7}{12} &= 8\frac{7}{12} \\ \hline 12\frac{15}{12} &= 13\frac{3}{12} = 13\frac{1}{4} \end{aligned}$	$\begin{aligned} 3\frac{7}{10} &= \\ +3\frac{4}{5} &= \\ \hline \end{aligned}$	$\begin{aligned} 6\frac{11}{18} &= \\ +2\frac{5}{9} &= \\ \hline \end{aligned}$

Add. Simplify.

a	b	c	d
1. $3\frac{2}{3} = 3\frac{8}{12}$	$5\frac{11}{12}$	$8\frac{3}{5}$	$4\frac{1}{2}$
$+3\frac{7}{12} = 3\frac{7}{12}$	$+7\frac{2}{3}$	$+4\frac{9}{20}$	$+2\frac{3}{4}$
$6\frac{15}{12} = 7\frac{1}{4}$			

a	b	c	d
2. $1\frac{3}{5}$	$5\frac{2}{3}$	$8\frac{3}{4}$	$5\frac{7}{8}$
$+4\frac{7}{10}$	$+3\frac{4}{9}$	$+5\frac{7}{16}$	$+6\frac{1}{4}$

a	b	c	d
3. $9\frac{3}{4}$	$4\frac{17}{20}$	$7\frac{8}{15}$	$7\frac{5}{6}$
$+2\frac{5}{12}$	$+5\frac{1}{4}$	$+3\frac{2}{3}$	$+4\frac{5}{18}$

a	b	c	d
4. $6\frac{2}{5}$	$12\frac{3}{8}$	$20\frac{5}{12}$	$1\frac{2}{3}$
$+4\frac{17}{20}$	$+\ 8\frac{3}{4}$	$+16\frac{3}{4}$	$+8\frac{7}{9}$

Line up the digits. Add. Simplify.

a	b	c
5. $6\frac{3}{4} + 2\frac{5}{8} =$ _____	$5\frac{4}{5} + 6\frac{7}{10} =$ _____	$7\frac{1}{2} + 4\frac{9}{14} =$ _____

a	b	c
6. $9\frac{7}{10} + 8\frac{1}{2} =$ _____	$12\frac{2}{7} + 2\frac{11}{14} =$ _____	$4\frac{5}{9} + 7\frac{2}{3} =$ _____

◈ MIXED PRACTICE

Multiply or divide.

a	b	c	d
1. 243	635	$5\overline{)2095}$	$60\overline{)30,690}$
$\times\ 29$	$\times\ 19$		

FRACTIONS AND MEASUREMENT

Subtraction of Mixed Numbers with Different Denominators

To subtract mixed numbers with different denominators, write the mixed numbers with like denominators. Subtract the fractions. Subtract the whole numbers. Simplify.

Find: $9\frac{11}{12} - 2\frac{1}{4}$

Write the mixed numbers with like denominators.	Subtract the fractions.	Subtract the whole numbers.	Simplify.
$9\frac{11}{12} = 9\frac{11}{12}$ $-2\frac{1}{4} = 2\frac{3}{12}$	$9\frac{11}{12} = 9\frac{11}{12}$ $-2\frac{1}{4} = 2\frac{3}{12}$ $\frac{8}{12}$	$9\frac{11}{12} = 9\frac{11}{12}$ $-2\frac{1}{4} = 2\frac{3}{12}$ $7\frac{8}{12}$	$7\frac{8}{12} = 7\frac{2}{3}$

GUIDED PRACTICE

Subtract. Simplify.

$\qquad a \qquad\qquad\qquad b \qquad\qquad\qquad c \qquad\qquad\qquad d$

1. $8\frac{5}{6} = 8\frac{5}{6}$ $\qquad$ $5\frac{3}{4} = 5\frac{3}{4}$ $\qquad$ $9\frac{5}{8} = 9\frac{5}{8}$ $\qquad$ $8\frac{7}{10} = 8\frac{7}{10}$

$-2\frac{1}{3} = 2\frac{2}{6}$ $\qquad$ $-3\frac{1}{2} = 3\frac{}{4}$ $\qquad$ $-3\frac{1}{4} = 3\frac{}{8}$ $\qquad$ $-1\frac{1}{2} = 1\frac{}{10}$

$\qquad\quad 6\frac{3}{6} = 6\frac{1}{2}$

2. $15\frac{3}{4} =$ $\qquad$ $16\frac{5}{6} =$ $\qquad$ $9\frac{5}{6} =$ $\qquad$ $12\frac{5}{8} =$

$-\ 8\frac{3}{8} =$ $\qquad$ $-10\frac{1}{2} =$ $\qquad$ $-6\frac{2}{3} =$ $\qquad$ $-\ 7\frac{1}{4} =$

3. $9\frac{1}{2} =$ $\qquad$ $3\frac{7}{8} =$ $\qquad$ $10\frac{3}{5} =$ $\qquad$ $8\frac{3}{4} =$

$-2\frac{1}{8} =$ $\qquad$ $-1\frac{1}{4} =$ $\qquad$ $-\ 4\frac{1}{10} =$ $\qquad$ $-6\frac{1}{8} =$

4. $3\frac{4}{9} =$ $\qquad$ $5\frac{6}{7} =$ $\qquad$ $4\frac{5}{12} =$ $\qquad$ $9\frac{7}{18} =$

$-1\frac{1}{3} =$ $\qquad$ $-2\frac{1}{14} =$ $\qquad$ $-3\frac{1}{4} =$ $\qquad$ $-6\frac{2}{9} =$

Subtract. Simplify.

	a	b	c	d
1.	$7\frac{7}{10}$	$11\frac{7}{10}$	$16\frac{3}{4}$	$9\frac{4}{5}$
	$-5\frac{2}{5}$	$-\;\;6\frac{1}{5}$	$-\;\;8\frac{1}{8}$	$-3\frac{1}{10}$
2.	$8\frac{1}{2}$	$12\frac{2}{3}$	$6\frac{3}{5}$	$10\frac{3}{4}$
	$-5\frac{1}{8}$	$-\;\;4\frac{1}{6}$	$-2\frac{3}{10}$	$-\;\;8\frac{5}{8}$
3.	$9\frac{3}{10}$	$7\frac{3}{4}$	$6\frac{4}{5}$	$12\frac{3}{4}$
	$-1\frac{1}{20}$	$-2\frac{3}{16}$	$-5\frac{4}{15}$	$-\;\;6\frac{1}{12}$
4.	$8\frac{4}{5}$	$12\frac{7}{8}$	$18\frac{5}{6}$	$15\frac{2}{3}$
	$-1\frac{7}{20}$	$-\;\;3\frac{3}{16}$	$-10\frac{5}{12}$	$-\;\;7\frac{5}{9}$

Line up the digits. Subtract. Simplify.

	a	b	c
5.	$15\frac{3}{4} - 8\frac{3}{8} =$ _____	$16\frac{5}{6} - 10\frac{1}{2} =$ _____	$8\frac{7}{10} - 1\frac{1}{2} =$ _____

$$15\frac{3}{4}$$
$$-\;8\frac{3}{8}$$
_____

	a	b	c
6.	$7\frac{3}{4} - 3\frac{3}{8} =$ _____	$10\frac{2}{5} - 6\frac{1}{10} =$ _____	$14\frac{3}{4} - 7\frac{5}{16} =$ _____

 MIXED PRACTICE

Find each answer.

	a	b	c	d
1.	408		325	8547
	$\times\;\;45$	$28\overline{)8456}$	98	-2073
			$+239$	

Subtraction of Fractions and Mixed Numbers
From Whole Numbers

Sometimes you will need to subtract a fraction from a whole number. To subtract from a whole number, write the whole number as a mixed number with a like denominator. Then subtract the fractions. Subtract the whole numbers.

Find: $6 - 4\frac{2}{3}$

To subtract, you need two fractions with like denominators.	Write 6 as a mixed number with 3 as the denominator.	Subtract the fractions.	Subtract the whole numbers.
$\begin{array}{r} 6 \\ -4\frac{2}{3} \\ \hline \end{array}$	$6 = 5 + \frac{3}{3} = 5\frac{3}{3}$ Remember: $\frac{3}{3} = 1$	$\begin{array}{r} 6 = 5\frac{3}{3} \\ -4\frac{2}{3} = 4\frac{2}{3} \\ \hline \frac{1}{3} \end{array}$	$\begin{array}{r} 6 = 5\frac{3}{3} \\ -4\frac{2}{3} = 4\frac{2}{3} \\ \hline 1\frac{1}{3} \end{array}$

GUIDED PRACTICE

Write each whole number as a mixed number.

	a	b	c	d
1.	$4 = 3 + \frac{6}{6} = 3\frac{6}{6}$	$6 = 5 + \frac{8}{} =$	$2 = 1 + \frac{}{3} =$	$7 = 6 + \frac{4}{} =$
2.	$10 = 9 + \frac{}{5} =$	$14 = 13 + \frac{}{3} =$	$9 = 8 + \frac{}{6} =$	$24 = 23 + \frac{}{4} =$

Subtract.

	a	b	c	d
3.	$\begin{array}{r} 9 = 8\frac{4}{4} \\ -2\frac{3}{4} = 2\frac{3}{4} \\ \hline 6\frac{1}{4} \end{array}$	$\begin{array}{r} 1\,2 = 11\frac{}{3} \\ -\ 5\frac{1}{3} = \ 5\frac{1}{3} \\ \hline \end{array}$	$\begin{array}{r} 9 = 8\frac{}{4} \\ -3\frac{1}{4} = 3\frac{1}{4} \\ \hline \end{array}$	$\begin{array}{r} 8 = 7\frac{}{8} \\ -1\frac{3}{8} = 1\frac{3}{8} \\ \hline \end{array}$
4.	$\begin{array}{r} 1\,4 = 13\frac{8}{8} \\ -\ 6\frac{3}{8} = 6\frac{3}{8} \\ \hline 7\frac{5}{8} \end{array}$	$\begin{array}{r} 2\,0 = \\ -\ 3\frac{7}{10} = \\ \hline \end{array}$	$\begin{array}{r} 1\,7 = \\ -\ 5\frac{2}{15} = \\ \hline \end{array}$	$\begin{array}{r} 1\,5 = \\ -\ 8\frac{5}{9} = \\ \hline \end{array}$
5.	$\begin{array}{r} 1\,2 = 11\frac{8}{8} \\ -\ \ \frac{5}{8} = \ \frac{5}{8} \\ \hline 11\frac{3}{8} \end{array}$	$\begin{array}{r} 5 = \\ -\ \frac{1}{6} = \\ \hline \end{array}$	$\begin{array}{r} 1\,3 = \\ -\ \frac{4}{9} = \\ \hline \end{array}$	$\begin{array}{r} 9 = \\ -\ \frac{3}{7} = \\ \hline \end{array}$

PRACTICE

Subtract.

	a	b	c	d
1.	9 $-\ \frac{3}{7}$	7 $-2\ \frac{5}{6}$	11 $-\ \ 3\ \frac{7}{8}$	10 $-\ \ 1\ \frac{1}{2}$
2.	22 $-16\ \frac{3}{5}$	18 $-\ \ \ \frac{7}{10}$	26 $-16\ \frac{7}{12}$	24 $-18\ \frac{5}{8}$
3.	16 $-\ \ \frac{2}{3}$	20 $-\ \ \frac{7}{8}$	19 $-13\ \frac{1}{2}$	23 $-\ \ 4\ \frac{3}{4}$

Line up the digits. Subtract.

    a   b   c

4. $12 - \frac{3}{8} =$ _____ $15 - 3\frac{4}{9} =$ _____ $9 - 7\frac{3}{8} =$ _____

12
$-\ \ \frac{3}{8}$

5. $19 - 12\frac{4}{15} =$ _____ $18 - 1\frac{3}{16} =$ _____ $9 - \frac{3}{10} =$ _____

MIXED PRACTICE

Estimate each sum or difference.

	a	b	c	d
1.	689 $+328$	550 -293	1497 $-\ \ 540$	2056 $+1870$

Estimate each product.

         a   b   c

2. $24 \times 395 =$ _____ $85 \times 207 =$ _____ $34 \times 56 =$ _____

Subtraction of Mixed Numbers with Regrouping

When subtracting mixed numbers, it may be necessary to regroup first. To regroup a mixed number for subtraction, write the whole number part as a mixed number. Add the mixed number and the fraction. Then subtract and simplify.

Find: $6\frac{5}{12} - 2\frac{3}{4}$

Write the fractions with like denominators. Compare the numerators.	$\frac{9}{12}$ is bigger than $\frac{5}{12}$. You can't subtract the fractions.	Add the mixed number and the fraction.	Subtract and simplify.
$6\frac{5}{12} = 6\frac{5}{12}$ $-2\frac{3}{4} = 2\frac{9}{12}$	To regroup $6\frac{5}{12}$, write 6 as a mixed number. $6 = 5\frac{12}{12}$	$6\frac{5}{12} = 5\frac{12}{12} + \frac{5}{12} = 5\frac{17}{12}$ note: $\frac{17}{12}$ is an improper fraction.	$6\frac{5}{12} = 5\frac{17}{12}$ $-2\frac{3}{4} = 2\frac{9}{12}$ $\overline{\qquad}$ $3\frac{8}{12} = 3\frac{2}{3}$

GUIDED PRACTICE

Regroup each mixed number.

	a	b	c
1.	$6\frac{1}{3} = 5\frac{3}{3} + \frac{1}{3} = 5\frac{4}{3}$	$8\frac{7}{8} = 7\frac{}{8}$	$9\frac{1}{6} = 8\frac{}{6}$
2.	$3\frac{6}{8} = 2\frac{}{8}$	$5\frac{9}{12} = 4\frac{}{12}$	$14\frac{8}{10} = 13\frac{}{10}$

Subtract. Simplify.

	a	b	c
3.	$9\frac{3}{8} = 9\frac{3}{8} = 8\frac{11}{8}$ $-4\frac{3}{4} = 4\frac{6}{8} = 4\frac{6}{8}$ $\overline{\qquad}$ $4\frac{5}{8}$	$7\frac{1}{3} = 7\frac{}{6} =$ $-2\frac{5}{6} = 2\frac{5}{6} =$	$9\frac{1}{5} = 9\frac{}{10} =$ $-2\frac{3}{10} = 2\frac{3}{10} =$
4.	$6\frac{3}{10}$ $-4\frac{2}{5}$	$13\frac{1}{4}$ $-6\frac{5}{8}$	$12\frac{5}{12}$ $-7\frac{2}{3}$
5.	$16\frac{4}{9}$ $-9\frac{2}{3}$	$18\frac{3}{10}$ $-7\frac{3}{5}$	$14\frac{1}{6}$ $-8\frac{1}{3}$

Subtract. Simplify.

	a	*b*	*c*
1.	$7\frac{5}{16}$ $-3\frac{7}{8}$	$9\frac{3}{8}$ $-4\frac{3}{4}$	$12\frac{1}{4}$ $-11\frac{5}{8}$
2.	$15\frac{1}{3}$ $-\ 4\frac{4}{9}$	$24\frac{1}{6}$ $-\ 3\frac{11}{12}$	$15\frac{3}{8}$ $-\ 7\frac{7}{16}$
3.	$15\frac{1}{6}$ $-\ 8\frac{1}{3}$	$24\frac{7}{16}$ $-13\frac{7}{8}$	$14\frac{1}{4}$ $-\ 6\frac{5}{8}$

Line up the digits. Subtract. Simplify.

          a   *b*   *c*

4. $16\frac{3}{10} - 9\frac{4}{5} = $ _____ $7\frac{1}{12} - 2\frac{1}{4} = $ _____ $12\frac{3}{8} - 6\frac{1}{2} = $ _____

$16\frac{3}{10}$

$-\ 9\frac{4}{5}$

5. $19\frac{1}{6} - 3\frac{2}{3} = $ _____ $27\frac{1}{5} - 23\frac{7}{15} = $ _____ $20\frac{3}{4} - 12\frac{11}{12} = $ _____

 MIXED PRACTICE

Multiply.

	a	*b*	*c*	*d*
1.	$4\ 1\ 6$ $\times 7\ 5\ 1$	$8\ 3\ 9$ $\times 7\ 7\ 2$	$1\ 8\ 8$ $\times 2\ 3\ 5$	$7\ 3\ 3$ $\times 5\ 1\ 8$

PROBLEM-SOLVING STRATEGY

Use Guess and Check

A good way to solve some problems is to guess the answer. Then check it and make another guess if necessary. Your next guess will be better because you will learn from the first guess. Then guess and check until you find the correct answer.

Read the problem.

Paul has 5 coins. Their total value is 62 cents. What coins and how many does he have? (Hint: make a table.)

Guess and check.

Decide what you already know. Paul must have at least two pennies if he has 62¢ in all.

Guess 1:		Check:
0 Quarters		There are too
6 Dimes	60¢	many coins.
0 Nickels		
<u>2 Pennies</u>	<u>2¢</u>	
8 coins	62¢	

Guess 2:		Check:
1 Quarter	25¢	The number of coins
2 Dimes	20¢	is correct, but the
0 Nickels		amount of money is not.
<u>2 Pennies</u>	<u>2¢</u>	
5 coins	47¢	

Guess 3:		Check:
2 Quarters	50¢	Both the number of
1 Dime	10¢	coins and the amount
0 Nickels		of money are correct.
<u>2 Pennies</u>	<u>2¢</u>	
5 coins	62¢	

So, Paul has 2 quarters, 1 dime, and 2 pennies.

Solve. Use guess and check.

1. Rita has 5 coins. Their total value is 31 cents. What coins and how many does she have?

Answer _____

2. The sum of Ron's age and Ray's age is 12. Ron is twice as old as Ray. How old are the boys?

Answer _____

3. Jane has 43 cents. She has 8 coins. Find the coins and the number of each that Jane has.

Answer _____

4. Caroline and Mark have 11 goldfish in all. Caroline has three more than Mark. How many fish do they each have?

Answer _____

5. Kendra is twice as old as Tim. In 10 years, Kendra will be four years older than Tim. How old are Kendra and Tim now?

Answer _____

6. The playground director has a total of 24 basketballs and footballs. He has 6 more footballs than basketballs. How many of each does he have?

Answer _____

Applications

Solve.

1. Cheryl went to the market to buy a chicken. The butcher weighed two chickens. One weighed $4\frac{1}{2}$ pounds; a second one weighed $3\frac{3}{4}$ pounds. How much less did the second one weigh?

   Answer _____

2. Indianapolis lies between St. Louis and Cleveland. From St. Louis to Indianapolis is $252\frac{1}{5}$ miles. It is $283\frac{2}{5}$ miles from Indianapolis to Cleveland. How far is it from St. Louis to Cleveland?

   Answer _____

3. From New York to Buffalo is $435\frac{9}{10}$ miles. From Buffalo to Chicago is $525\frac{3}{10}$ miles. How many miles is it from New York to Chicago?

   Answer _____

4. Frederic weighed $156\frac{1}{6}$ pounds in February. In April he weighed $143\frac{1}{3}$ pounds. How much less did he weigh in April?

   Answer _____

5. Matthew went fishing and caught a bass weighing $3\frac{1}{2}$ pounds. Then he caught another that weighed $4\frac{1}{4}$ pounds. How much heavier was the second fish?

   Answer _____

6. Alice is $64\frac{1}{2}$ inches tall, and Mabel is $61\frac{1}{2}$ inches tall. How much taller is Alice than Mabel?

   Answer _____

7. Joe weighs $174\frac{1}{8}$ pounds. Charles weighs $179\frac{1}{2}$ pounds. Charles weighs how much more than Joe?

   Answer _____

8. A storekeeper sold $29\frac{1}{2}$ yards of material from a bolt of cloth that contained 60 yards. How many yards of the material were left?

   Answer _____

FRACTIONS AND MEASUREMENT

Customary Length

The customary units that are used to measure length are inch, foot, yard, and mile. The chart gives the relationship of one unit to another.

- A business envelope is about 10 inches long.
- A basketball hoop is 10 feet high.

larger ← ⬜ → smaller

1 foot (ft) = 12 inches (in.)
1 yard (yd) = 3 ft   = 36 in.
1 mile (mi) = 1760 yd   = 5280 ft

Find: 5 yd = _____ ft

To change yards to a smaller unit, multiply.

1 yd = 3 ft
5 × 3 = 15
5 yd = 15 ft

You will have more feet.

Find: 18 in. = _____ ft

To change inches to a larger unit, divide.

12 in. = 1 ft
$18 ÷ 12 = 1\frac{6}{12}$ or $1\frac{1}{2}$
18 in. = $1\frac{1}{2}$ ft

You will have fewer feet.

PRACTICE

How would you measure the following? Use in., ft, yd or mi.

a

1. length of a new pencil _____

2. width of a kitchen table _____

3. height of a bicycle _____

b

height of a telephone pole _____

length of a football field _____

length of a hiking trail _____

Use the chart to complete the following.

a	b	c
4. 36 in. = _____ yd	12 in. = _____ ft	1 yd = _____ ft
5. 1760 yd = _____ mi	1 yd = _____ in.	1 mi = _____ ft
6. 3 ft = _____ yd	1 mi = _____ yd	1 ft = _____ in.

Change each measurement to the smaller unit.

a	b	c
7. 7 ft = __84__ in.	15 yd = _____ ft	3 mi = _____ ft

Change each measurement to the larger unit.

a	b	c
8. 42 in. = __$3\frac{1}{2}$__ ft	72 in. = _____ yd	7040 yd = _____ mi

89

Customary Weight

The customary units that are used to measure weight are ounce, pound, and ton. The chart shows the relationship of one unit to another.

| 1 pound (lb) = 16 ounces (oz) |
| 1 ton (T) = 2000 pounds |

• A stick of margarine weighs 4 ounces.
• A small loaf of bread weighs about **1** pound.

Find: 3 lb = _____ oz

> To change pounds to a smaller unit, multiply.
>
> 1 lb = 16 oz
> 3 × 16 = 48
> 3 lb = 48 oz
>
> You will have more ounces.

Find: 5000 lb = _____ T

> To change pounds to a larger unit, divide.
>
> 2000 lb = 1 T
> $5000 \div 2000 = 2\frac{1}{2}$
> $5000 \text{ lb} = 2\frac{1}{2} \text{ T}$
>
> You will have fewer tons.

PRACTICE

How would you measure the following? Use oz, lb, or T.

	a	*b*
1.	weight of a cat _____	weight of a pick-up truck _____
2.	weight of a tennis ball _____	weight of a tiger _____
3.	weight of a bag of potatoes _____	weight of a baby _____

Use the chart to complete the following.

	a	*b*	*c*
4.	16 oz = ___1___ lb	2000 lb = _____ T	1 lb = _____ oz

Change each measurement to the smaller unit.

	a	*b*	*c*
5.	5 lb = ___80___ oz	2 T = _____ lb	2 lb = _____ oz
6.	7 T = _____ lb	6 lb = _____ oz	9 lb = _____ oz

Change each measurement to the larger unit.

	a	*b*	*c*
7.	24 oz = ___$1\frac{1}{2}$___ lb	6000 lb = _____ T	3000 lb = _____ T
8.	36 oz = _____ lb	92 oz = _____ lb	50 oz = _____ lb

FRACTIONS AND MEASUREMENT

Customary Capacity

The customary units that are used to measure capacity are cup, pint, quart, and gallon. The chart shows the relationship of one unit to another.

- A drinking glass holds 1 cup of liquid.
- A small pan for cooking holds 1 quart.
- A large water pitcher holds 1 gallon.

1 pint (pt) = 2 cups (c)
1 quart (qt) = 2 pt
= 4 c
1 gallon (gal) = 4 qt
= 8 pt
= 16 c

Find: 7 qt = _____ pt

To change quarts to a smaller unit, multiply.

$$1 \text{ qt} = 2 \text{ pt}$$
$$7 \times 2 = 14$$
$$7 \text{ qt} = 14 \text{ pt}$$

You will have more pints.

Find: 10 pt = _____ gal

To change pints to a larger unit, divide.

$$8 \text{ pt} = 1 \text{ gal}$$
$$10 \div 8 = 1\frac{2}{8} \text{ or } 1\frac{1}{4}$$
$$10 \text{ pt} = 1\frac{1}{4} \text{ gal}$$

You will have fewer gallons.

PRACTICE

How would you measure the following? Use c, pt, qt, or gal.

a b

1. capacity of a large milk container _____   capacity of a coffee mug _____

2. capacity of a tea pot _____   capacity of a fish tank _____

3. capacity of a pail _____   capacity of a cereal bowl _____

Use the chart to complete the following.

a	b	c
4. 2 c = _____ pt	2 pt = _____ qt	4 qt = _____ gal
5. 1 gal = _____ c	4 c = _____ qt	8 pt = _____ gal
6. 1 qt = _____ pt	16 c = _____ gal	1 pt = _____ c

Change each measurement to the smaller unit.

a	b	c
7. 7 qt = _____ c	3 gal = _____ c	8 pt = _____ c

Change each measurement to the larger unit.

a	b	c
8. 24 c = $1\frac{1}{2}$ gal	12 c = _____ qt	8 qt = _____ gal

91

PROBLEM SOLVING

Applications

Solve.

1. Lupe walked 4290 feet. How much less than a mile did she walk? (5280 ft = 1 mi)

Answer _____

2. The Browns use 3 quarts of milk each day. How many quarts of milk do they use in two weeks?

Answer _____

3. Pauline has driven her car 5589 miles. How many gallons of gas has she used if she gets 23 miles to the gallon?

Answer _____

4. A freight train has 65 boxcars. The average load in each boxcar is 28 tons. What is the total load carried in the boxcars?

Answer _____

5. Frank weighs $102\frac{1}{2}$ pounds and Peter weighs $89\frac{1}{4}$ pounds. How much more does Frank weigh than Peter?

Answer _____

6. The department store received a shipment of toys. Each box weighed about 60 pounds. How many boxes would be in a shipment that weighed 42,000 pounds?

Answer _____

7. Cindy lives between Fay and Pedro. Fay lives $\frac{7}{8}$ mile from Cindy. Pedro lives $\frac{5}{16}$ mile from Cindy. How many miles from Pedro does Fay live?

Answer _____

8. Esther needs $2\frac{5}{8}$ yards of lace for trimming a dress and $1\frac{3}{4}$ yards for a blouse. How many yards does she need altogether?

Answer _____

9. The distance from Chicago to Milwaukee is 85 miles. The distance from Milwaukee to St. Paul is 325 miles. How far is it from Chicago to St. Paul?

Answer _____

10. The rainfall for June was $7\frac{9}{10}$ inches. In July $7\frac{3}{10}$ inches of rain fell. How much more rain fell in June than in July?

Answer _____

PROBLEM SOLVING

Applications

Solve.

1. There are 3 feet in a yard. How many yards of fencing are needed for one side of a park which measures 528 feet?

   Answer _____

2. Ramos has a 7-foot board. He will use it to make a shelf $4\frac{2}{3}$ feet long. How much of the board will not be used?

   Answer _____

3. Sara drove 576 miles on her vacation. Nicole drove 259 miles. How many more miles did Sara drive than Nicole?

   Answer _____

4. Dick's recipe uses 2 cups of flour for 12 muffins. How many cups of flour does he need for 24 muffins?

   Answer _____

5. Barry counted 47 boxes of books on a truck. The total weight of the boxes was 4653 pounds. What was the average weight of each box?

   Answer _____

6. Martha caught one fish weighing $2\frac{3}{4}$ pounds and another fish weighing $1\frac{1}{2}$ pounds. How much did the two fish weigh in all?

   Answer _____

7. Jason lives in the country. Each day he rides 38 miles on the bus. How many miles does he ride in 6 days?

   Answer _____

8. Frances is $63\frac{1}{4}$ inches tall. Grace is $3\frac{3}{4}$ inches shorter than Frances. How tall is Grace?

   Answer _____

9. A grocery store sold 379 gallons of milk on Monday and 286 gallons of milk on Tuesday. How many gallons of milk were sold on those two days?

   Answer _____

10. One Saturday the Scouts hiked $3\frac{1}{8}$ miles in the morning. They hiked $2\frac{7}{8}$ miles in the afternoon. How far did the Scouts hike in all?

    Answer _____

Use a Formula

The facts in a problem may be related by a formula. Below are listed some commonly used formulas and an explanation for each.

$A = l \times w$ (Area of a rectangle = length × width)
Area is the number of square units inside a figure. The area of this square is 6 units.

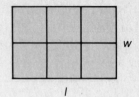

$P = 2l + 2w$ (Perimeter of a rectangle = 2 × the length + 2 × the width)
Perimeter is the distance around a figure. The perimeter of this rectangle is 14 units.

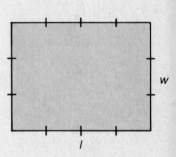

$P = 4 \times s$ (Perimeter of a square = 4 × the measure of a side)
The perimeter of this square is 12 units.

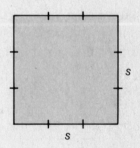

To use a formula, copy the formula and substitute the numbers you have been given. Then solve.

Read the problem.

Oscar's basement is 30 feet long and 25 feet wide. What is the area of the basement?

Select a formula.

Use the formula for area of a rectangle.
$A = l \times w$

Substitute the numbers.

Replace l and w with the numbers given.
$A = l \times w$
$A = 30 \times 25$

Solve the problem.

$A = 750$
The area of the basement is 750 square feet.

Solve. Use one of the formulas given in the chart.

1. A rectangle is 5 feet long and 3 feet wide. Find its perimeter in feet.

Answer _____

2. A square has a side that measures 8 inches. Find its perimeter in inches.

Answer _____

3. The floor of Kim's room measures 13 feet in length and 11 feet in width. How many square feet of carpet does Kim need to cover her floor? (Find area.)

Answer _____

4. Sam wants to put a fence around his garden. The garden is 6 yards long and 4 yards wide. How many yards of fencing should he order? (Find perimeter.)

Answer _____

5. Emily wants to put trim around a square window that measures 3 feet on each side. How many feet of trim does she need? (Find perimeter.)

Answer _____

6. Jacob wants to wallpaper one wall of his room. The wall measures 12 feet in length and 8 feet in width. How many square feet of wallpaper does Jacob need to cover the wall? (Find area.)

Answer _____

Unit 5 Review

Add. Simplify.

a	b	c	d
1. $5\frac{1}{8}$	$6\frac{5}{9}$	$10\frac{3}{10}$	$8\frac{1}{6}$
$+3\frac{1}{2}$	$+9\frac{1}{3}$	$+\ 4\frac{2}{5}$	$+18\frac{2}{3}$

2. $3\frac{5}{8}$	$10\frac{3}{5}$	$8\frac{7}{15}$	$11\frac{5}{6}$
$+6\frac{3}{4}$	$+\ 6\frac{9}{10}$	$+\ 4\frac{2}{3}$	$+\ 9\frac{2}{3}$

Subtract. Simplify.

a	b	c	d
3. $10\frac{7}{8}$	$16\frac{15}{16}$	$9\frac{2}{3}$	$18\frac{5}{6}$
$-\ 4\frac{3}{4}$	$-\ 5\frac{5}{8}$	$-1\frac{2}{9}$	$-12\frac{1}{2}$

Regroup each whole number as a mixed number.

a	b	c	d
4. $10 = 9\frac{}{8}$	$18 = 17\frac{}{6}$	$9 = 8\frac{}{12}$	$7 = 6\frac{}{10}$

Subtract.

a	b	c	d
5. 13	15	18	16
$-\ \ \frac{5}{6}$	$-\ \ \frac{1}{3}$	$-\ 3\frac{4}{7}$	$-\ 8\frac{3}{8}$

Regroup each mixed number.

a	b	c	d
6. $5\frac{2}{4} = 4\frac{}{4}$	$7\frac{5}{8} = 6\frac{}{8}$	$10\frac{6}{9} = 9\frac{}{9}$	$12\frac{3}{15} = 11\frac{}{15}$

Subtract. Simplify.

a	b	c	d
7. $15\frac{1}{3}$	$20\frac{3}{8}$	$11\frac{3}{10}$	$14\frac{4}{15}$
$-\ 8\frac{5}{6}$	$-12\frac{3}{4}$	$-\ 5\frac{4}{5}$	$-\ 8\frac{2}{3}$

FRACTIONS AND MEASUREMENT
Unit 5 Review

How would you measure the following? Use in., ft, or mi.

	a	*b*
1.	length of a shoe _____	length of a wagon _____

How would you measure the following? Use oz, lb, or T.

	a	*b*
2.	weight of a dog _____	weight of a truck _____

How would you measure the following? Use c, pt, qt, or gal.

	a	*b*
3.	capacity of a swimming pool _____	capacity of a coffee maker _____

Change each measurement to the smaller unit.

	a	*b*	*c*
4.	3 yd = _____ in.	7 pt = _____ c	5 yd = _____ ft
5.	4 gal = _____ pt	5 ft = _____ in.	4 lb = _____ oz

Change each measurement to the larger unit.

	a	*b*	*c*
6.	4000 lb = _____ T	48 in. = _____ ft	10 pt = _____ qt
7.	9 c = _____ qt	12 qt = _____ gal	9 ft = _____ yd

Solve these problems.

8. Jack can jump $7\frac{1}{2}$ feet. Jim can jump $6\frac{1}{4}$ feet. How much farther can Jack jump than Jim?

Answer _____

9. The circus has 27 elephants. Together these elephants weigh 35,100 pounds. What is the average weight of each elephant?

Answer _____

10. A crew loaded a truck with 125 sacks of potatoes. Each sack weighs 75 pounds. How many pounds of potatoes were on the truck?

Answer _____

11. Sue needs $3\frac{2}{3}$ yards of canvas for her pup tent and $2\frac{2}{3}$ yards for her bedroll. How many yards of canvas does she need in all?

Answer _____

Meaning of Decimals

Like fractions, decimals show parts of a whole. The shaded portion of each picture can be written as a fraction or as a decimal.

 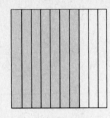 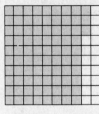 

$\frac{1}{1}$ or 1

Read: one

$\frac{7}{10}$ or 0.7

seven tenths

$\frac{83}{100}$ or 0.83

eighty-three hundredths

$1\frac{5}{10}$ or 1.5

one and five tenths

Remember,
- a decimal point separates a whole number and its decimal parts.
- a whole number has a decimal point but it is usually not written. 2 is the same as 2.0.
- a decimal point is read as "and".

PRACTICE

Write the decimal shown by the shaded part of each figure.

     a   *b*   *c*

1.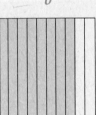

   _____   _____   _____

2.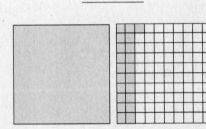

   _____   _____   _____

Write each money amount with a dollar sign and a decimal point.

    a   *b*   *c*

3. one dollar __*$1.00*__ ten cents __*$0.10*__ one penny __*$0.01*__

4. twelve dollars _____ three dimes _____ eight pennies _____

5. five dollars and eleven

 cents _____   thirty-seven cents _____ sixty-four cents _____

Decimal Place Value

You can use a place-value chart to help you understand decimal places. The digits to the right of the decimal point show decimals. The digits to the left of the decimal point show whole numbers.

The 2 is in the tens place.
Its value is 20 or 2 tens.

The 8 is in the ones place.
Its value is 8 or 8 ones.

The 6 is in the tenths place.
Its value is 0.6 or 6 tenths.

The 0 is in the hundredths place.
Its value is 0 or 0 hundredths.

The 3 is in the thousandths place.
Its value is 0.003 or 3 thousandths.

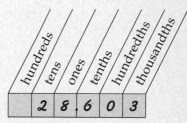

←whole numbers . decimals→

PRACTICE

Write each number in the place-value chart.

1. 29.01
2. 0.485
3. 3.782
4. 67.567
5. 10.0
6. 142.04

Write the place name for the 7 in each number.

	a	b	c
7.	2.73 _____tenths_____	8.076 _____	12.687 _____
8.	0.017 _____	7.019 _____	6.007 _____
9.	10.47 _____	70.480 _____	0.760 _____

Write the value of the underlined digit.

	a	b	c
10.	0.22<u>3</u> __3 thousandths__	0.1<u>9</u>4 _____	0.60<u>4</u> _____
11.	1.9<u>5</u> _____	<u>3</u>.008 _____	0.1<u>8</u> _____
12.	6<u>4</u>.5 _____	4.67<u>8</u> _____	<u>1</u>6.96 _____

WORKING WITH DECIMALS

Reading and Writing Decimals

A place-value chart can help you understand how to read and write decimals.

To read a decimal, read as a whole number.
Then name the place value of the last digit.

Read 0.79 as seventy-nine hundredths.

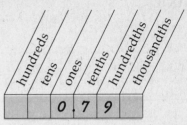

To read a decimal that has a whole number part,
- read the whole number part.
- read the decimal point as "and".
- read the decimal part as a whole number and then name the place value of the last digit.

Read 35.206 as thirty-five and two hundred six thousandths.

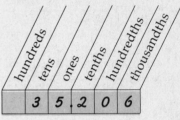

GUIDED PRACTICE

Write the place value of the last digit of the number.

	a	b	c
1. 3.09	_hundredths_	89.065 _____	0.4 _____
2. 12.1 _____		2.63 _____	4.002 _____
3. 0.4 _____		64.002 _____	640.20 _____

Write as a decimal.

	a	b
4. four tenths	_0.4_	four hundredths _____
5. four thousandths _____		five hundred four thousandths _____
6. sixteen thousandths _____		sixteen hundredths _____
7. ten and thirteen hundredths _____		fifty-four and one hundredth _____

Write each decimal in words.

8. 0.048 _forty-eight thousandths_ _____

9. 0.64 _____

10. 9.4 _____

11. 130.70 _____

12. 1.532 _____

Write as a decimal.

a	*b*
1. five tenths _____	eighty-nine hundredths _____
2. three and four thousandths _____	sixty-three hundredths _____
3. four and seven tenths _____	eight and five hundredths _____
4. thirty-one hundredths _____	twenty-eight thousandths _____
5. two and three hundredths _____	fourteen hundredths _____
6. sixty and four tenths _____	five and six tenths _____
7. seventeen thousandths _____	eight and nine thousandths _____
8. nine and nine hundredths _____	twenty-three hundredths _____
9. seventy and one tenth _____	seventy-one hundredths _____

Write each decimal in words.

10. 0.23 _____

11. 0.8 _____

12. 4.53 _____

13. 6.009 _____

14. 9.802 _____

15. 5.075 _____

16. 7.5 _____

17. 18.04 _____

18. 0.18 _____

 MIXED PRACTICE

Line up the digits. Then find each answer.

a	*b*	*c*
1. 3560 − 2684 = _____	765 + 1258 + 584 = _____	812 × 62 = _____
2. 26,096 − 1878 = _____	408,341 + 62,889 = _____	6049 ÷ 36 = _____

Compare and Order Decimals

To compare two decimal numbers, begin at the left.
Compare the digits in each place.

The symbol > means "is greater than."   1.9 > 1.2
The symbol < means "is less than."   3.1 < 3.5
The symbol = means "is equal to."   2.7 = 2.70

Compare: 1.5 and 1.4

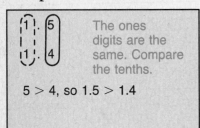

The ones digits are the same. Compare the tenths.

5 > 4, so 1.5 > 1.4

Compare: $0.06 and $0.31

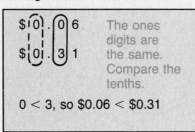

The ones digits are the same. Compare the tenths.

0 < 3, so $0.06 < $0.31

Compare: 0.2 and 0.29

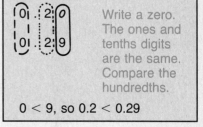

Write a zero. The ones and tenths digits are the same. Compare the hundredths.

0 < 9, so 0.2 < 0.29

GUIDED PRACTICE

Compare. Write >, <, or =.

	a	b	c
1.	1.5 __<__ 1.9	1.3 _____ 1.8	3.5 _____ 3.3
	1 . 5	1 . 3	3 . 5
	1 . 9	1 . 8	3 . 3
2.	$1.76 _____ $1.92	$0.38 _____ $0.56	$8.62 _____ $8.27
	$ 1 . 7 6	$ 0 . 3 8	8 . 6 2
	$ 1 . 9 2	$ 0 . 5 6	8 . 2 7
3.	0.49 _____ 0.490	0.890 _____ 0.089	0.134 _____ 0.143
	0 . 4 9	0 . 8 9 0	0 . 1 3 4
	0 . 4 9 0	0 . 0 8 9	0 . 1 4 3

Write in order from least to greatest.

	a	b
4.	14.0 1.4 140 _____	0.7 0.007 0.07 _____
	1 4 . 0	
	1 . 4	
	1 4 0	
5.	345 3.45 34.5 _____	0.80 0.79 0.81 _____

Compare. Write <, >, or =.

	a	b	c
1.	6.210 _____ 6.201	$19.78 _____ $19.87	58.9 _____ 59.0
2.	117.8 _____ 171.8	0.609 _____ 0.61	44.8 _____ 44.80
3.	6 _____ 6.0	27.9 _____ 2.79	15.34 _____ 5.434
4.	0.89 _____ 0.009	0.9 _____ 0.89	$0.09 _____ $0.89
5.	61.4 _____ 61.40	6.315 _____ 6.31	200.0 _____ 200
6.	165 _____ 165.001	12.385 _____ 12.3	2.428 _____ 2.43

Write in order from least to greatest.

	a	b
7.	$17.0 $1.70 $170 _____	0.06 0.60 0.066 _____
8.	5.6 5.06 5.602 _____	0.3 0.003 0.03 _____
9.	1.2 21 2.1 _____	0.090 0.8 0.007 _____

 MIXED PRACTICE

Write as a mixed number.

	a	b	c	d
1.	$\frac{35}{3} =$ _____	$\frac{39}{4} =$ _____	$\frac{27}{2} =$ _____	$\frac{29}{4} =$ _____

Add or subtract. Simplify.

	a	b	c
2.	$\frac{1}{3} + \frac{1}{3} =$ _____	$\frac{7}{8} - \frac{1}{4} =$ _____	$\frac{1}{2} + \frac{3}{8} =$ _____
3.	$2\frac{1}{3} + 1\frac{1}{6} =$ _____	$5\frac{1}{4} + 3\frac{1}{8} =$ _____	$6\frac{1}{2} - 2\frac{3}{8} =$ _____

PROBLEM-SOLVING STRATEGY
Make a List

Sometimes it helps to make a list to solve a problem. When you put information in a list in an organized way, it is easy to see how to solve the problem.

Read the problem.

Leroy, Dave, and Tom are having a race. They wonder about the different ways they can finish in first place, second place, and third place. How many different race results are there?

Make a list.

To make a list, start by writing one of the boys in first place. Then determine how many ways for the other boys to finish second and third. Repeat with each of the boys in first place.

First Place	Second Place	Third Place
Leroy	Dave	Tom
Leroy	Tom	Dave
Dave	Leroy	Tom
Dave	Tom	Leroy
Tom	Leroy	Dave
Tom	Dave	Leroy

Solve the problem.

Count the possible race results. It is easy to see the six possible ways the three boys could finish the race.

Make a list. Use your list to solve each problem.

1. Suppose you have 5 index cards. Each card has one of these numbers on it: 1, 2, 3, 4, or 5. How many different two-digit numbers can you make with these cards?

Answer _____

2. Gail, Pam, Lena, and Ramon sit in the first row. In how many different ways can they be seated if there are four seats in the row?

Answer _____

3. Dawn has a blue pen and a black pen. She has a green notebook, a brown notebook, a red notebook, and a purple notebook. In how many different ways can she choose a pen and a notebook?

Answer _____

4. A cafeteria offers tomato soup or pea soup served with saltines or sesame crackers. How many soup and cracker combinations are there?

Answer _____

Applications

Solve.

1. Sandra bought one and four tenths pounds of broccoli. Carl bought one and thirty-eight hundredths pounds of broccoli. Which person bought more broccoli?

Answer _____

2. Jerome's bicycle odometer shows two hundred fifty-one and nine hundredths miles. Richard's bicycle odometer shows two hundred fifty and ninety-seven hundredths miles. Which person's bike has gone further?

Answer _____

3. Lucas jumped 446.53 centimeters in the school championship. When the newspaper reported his long jump, the number had been rounded to the nearest tenth. According to the newspaper, what was the length of Lucas' jump?

Answer _____

4. Linda drives 13.8 miles to work. When she records the distance in her mileage book, she rounds the number to the nearest one. What number does Linda write in her book?

Answer _____

5. Reggie received a paycheck for $147.38. Write the amount of the check in words.

Answer _____

6. Kendra had a mineral sample that weighed seventy-seven hundredths of a gram. Write the amount of her sample using digits.

Answer _____

7. In one day, Washington, D.C. had one and twenty-eight hundredths inches of rain. On that same day, Montgomery, Alabama had one and twenty-six hundredths inches of rain. Which city had more rain on that day?

Answer _____

8. In one day, Syracuse had 0.09 inches of rain. On that same day, Lexington had 0.10 inches of rain. Which city had more rain on that day?

Answer _____

WORKING WITH DECIMALS

Rounding Decimals

Rounding decimals can be used to tell about how many. You can use a number line to round decimals.

Remember, when a number is halfway, always round up.

Round 42.3 to the nearest one.

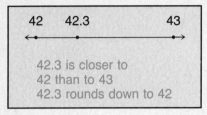

42.3 is closer to
42 than to 43
42.3 rounds down to 42

Round $5.78 to the nearest dollar.

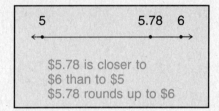

$5.78 is closer to
$6 than to $5
$5.78 rounds up to $6

Round 7.25 to the nearest tenth.

| 7.2 | 7.25 | 7.3 |

7.25 is halfway between
7.2 and 7.3
7.25 rounds up to 7.3

PRACTICE

Round to the nearest one.

	a	b	c	d
1.	3.8 ___4___	2.5 _____	1.9 _____	7.3 _____
2.	32.4 _____	40.6 _____	33.9 _____	62.7 _____
3.	39.6 ___40___	82.3 _____	78.9 _____	50.5 _____
4.	6.78 _____	2.05 _____	3.29 _____	9.36 _____

Round each amount to the nearest dollar.

	a	b	c	d
5.	$2.81 _____	$14.36 _____	$8.90 _____	$5.25 _____
6.	$9.15 _____	$3.67 _____	$1.42 _____	$73.07 _____
7.	$312.52 _____	$7.99 _____	$0.36 _____	$40.02 _____
8.	$0.98 _____	$3.49 _____	$10.10 _____	$25.50 _____

Round to the nearest tenth.

	a	b	c	d
9.	0.36 ___0.4___	0.72 _____	0.83 _____	0.45 _____
10.	6.29 _____	9.07 _____	4.56 _____	7.41 _____
11.	82.78 _____	29.93 _____	85.54 _____	60.04 _____
12.	79.98 ___80___	57.72 _____	60.59 _____	30.51 _____

PROBLEM-SOLVING STRATEGY

Use Estimation

Many problems can be solved by estimation. Often, you do not need an exact answer to solve a problem. An estimate is found by rounding some or all of the numbers and then doing mental math. Mental math is computing an answer in your head.

Read the problem.

Daniel has $32 to spend on some T-shirts for summer camp. T-shirts cost $4.75 each. Can Daniel buy 7 T-shirts?

Identify the important facts.

T-shirts cost $4.75 each.

Daniel wants to buy 7 T-shirts.

He has $32 to spend.

Round.

$4.75 can be rounded to $5.

Solve the problem.

Think: $5 \times 7 = ?$
$5 \times 7 = 35

$35 is more than $32, so Daniel cannot buy 7 T-shirts.

Use estimation to solve each problem.

1. 42,739 people live in Oakdale and 38,256 people live in Cedarville. About how many more people live in Oakdale than in Cedarville?

2. The Jacksons drove 381 miles from their house to San Diego. They followed the same route back home. About how far did they travel in all?

Estimate _____

Estimate _____

Use estimation to solve each problem. (Hint: Round decimals to the nearest one.)

3. Tickets to the circus cost $6.50 each. The Scout troop raised $60. Can all 8 members of the troop go to the circus?

Estimate _____

Yes or No? _____

4. The school auditorium seats 600 people. If 277 students and 205 parents attended the spring concert, was every seat in the auditorium occupied?

Estimate _____

Yes or No? _____

5. The school cafeteria served 285 hot lunches and 394 sandwich plates. About how many meals were served in all?

Estimate _____

6. The members of a hiking club planned a three-day trip. They planned to hike 5850 meters the first day, 7120 meters the second day, and 6430 meters the third day. About how many meters do they plan to hike?

Estimate _____

7. Frank bought 4 rolls of wrapping paper for $3.75 each. Regina bought 5 rolls of wrapping paper for $2.98 each. Who paid less in all for the wrapping paper?

Estimate _____

Answer _____

8. Carmelita sold 23 tickets for a concert. Each ticket cost $18. Her goal was $300 in ticket sales. Did she reach her goal?

Estimate _____

Yes or No? _____

109

Fraction and Decimal Equivalents

Sometimes you will need to either change a decimal to a fraction or a fraction to a decimal.

To write a decimal as a fraction, identify the value of the last place in the decimal. Use this place value to write the denominator.

Decimal		Fraction or Mixed Number
0.7	=	$\frac{7}{10}$
0.59	=	$\frac{59}{100}$
0.005	=	$\frac{5}{1000}$
3.47	=	$3\frac{47}{100}$ or $\frac{347}{100}$

To write a fraction that has a denominator of 10, 100, or 1000 as a decimal, write the digits from the numerator. Then write the decimal point.

Fraction or Mixed Number		Decimal
$\frac{3}{10}$	=	0.3
$\frac{43}{100}$	=	0.43
$\frac{529}{1000}$	=	0.529
$\frac{618}{100}$ or $6\frac{18}{100}$	=	6.18

PRACTICE

Write each decimal as a fraction.

	a	b	c	d
1.	0.3 $\frac{3}{10}$	0.7 _____	0.9 _____	0.1 _____
2.	0.03 $\frac{3}{100}$	0.07 _____	0.09 _____	0.01 _____

Write each decimal as a mixed number.

	a	b	c	d
3.	2.3 $2\frac{3}{10}$	6.9 _____	3.7 _____	8.1 _____
4.	9.88 $9\frac{88}{100}$	5.07 _____	4.90 _____	2.25 _____

Write each fraction as a decimal.

	a	b	c	d
5.	$\frac{4}{10}$ 0.4	$\frac{8}{10}$ _____	$\frac{6}{10}$ _____	$\frac{2}{10}$ _____
6.	$\frac{23}{100}$ 0.23	$\frac{97}{100}$ _____	$\frac{246}{1000}$ _____	$\frac{810}{1000}$ _____
7.	$\frac{51}{10}$ $5\frac{1}{10} = 5.1$	$\frac{27}{10}$ _____	$\frac{38}{10}$ _____	$\frac{94}{10}$ _____
8.	$\frac{306}{100}$ $3\frac{06}{100} = 3.06$	$\frac{901}{100}$ _____	$\frac{8825}{1000}$ _____	$\frac{6975}{1000}$ _____

WORKING WITH DECIMALS

Fraction and Decimal Equivalents

Not all fractions can be changed to decimal form easily. To write fractions that have denominators other than 10, 100, or 1000 as decimals, first write an equivalent fraction that has a denominator of 10, 100, or 1000. Then write the equivalent fraction as a decimal.

Remember, not all fractions have simple decimal equivalents.

Examples: $\frac{1}{3} = 0.333\ldots$ $\frac{1}{6} = 0.166\ldots$

Write $\frac{1}{2}$ as a decimal.

Write $\frac{1}{2}$ with 10 as the denominator.	Write the fraction as a decimal.
$\frac{1}{2} = \frac{1 \times 5}{2 \times 5} = \frac{5}{10}$	$= 0.5$

Write $3\frac{1}{4}$ as a decimal.

Write $3\frac{1}{4}$ as an improper fraction.	Write the new fraction with 100 as the denominator.	Write the fraction as a decimal.
$3\frac{1}{4} = \frac{13}{4}$	$\frac{13}{4} = \frac{13 \times 25}{4 \times 25} = \frac{325}{100}$	$= 3.25$

PRACTICE

Write each fraction as a decimal.

	a	b	c
1.	$\frac{3}{4} = \frac{3 \times 25}{4 \times 25} = \frac{75}{100} = 0.75$	$\frac{1}{5} =$	$\frac{24}{25} =$
2.	$\frac{4}{5} =$	$\frac{7}{20} =$	$\frac{3}{20} =$
3.	$\frac{6}{25} =$	$\frac{10}{20} =$	$\frac{13}{25} =$
4.	$\frac{17}{5} = \frac{17 \times 2}{5 \times 2} = \frac{34}{10} = 3.4$	$\frac{9}{2} =$	$\frac{51}{20} =$
5.	$\frac{68}{25} =$	$\frac{33}{4} =$	$\frac{34}{5} =$

Write each mixed number as a decimal.

	a	b
6.	$4\frac{3}{20} = \frac{83}{20} = \frac{83 \times 5}{20 \times 5} = \frac{415}{100} = 4.15$	$20\frac{1}{5} =$
7.	$3\frac{2}{25} =$	$11\frac{1}{2} =$
8.	$7\frac{9}{20} =$	$5\frac{21}{25} =$

PROBLEM SOLVING

Applications

Solve.

1. Wanda ran for $\frac{1}{2}$ hour. Sue ran for 0.6 hour. Which person ran for a longer period of time?

Answer _____

2. Carlos threw a ball 12.01 meters. Linda threw a ball 12.0 meters. Which person threw the ball farther?

Answer _____

3. David walked $19\frac{1}{2}$ meters in one minute. Maria walked 19.57 meters in one minute. Which person walked farther in one minute?

Answer _____

4. Elisa needed $\frac{3}{5}$ yard of fabric. Marybeth needed 0.5 yards of fabric. Which person needed more fabric?

Answer _____

5. Robert spent $\frac{3}{5}$ of a day driving. Write this amount as a decimal.

Answer _____

6. Roger spent thirty-six dollars and forty-two cents on new shoes. Write this amount as a decimal.

Answer _____

7. Clarence wrote a check for $23.32. Write this amount in words.

Answer _____

8. At store A, milk costs a dollar and a quarter. At store B, the same amount of milk costs $1.37. At which store does milk cost the least?

Answer _____

Unit 6 Review

Write the place name for the 8 in each number.

a	b	c
1. 0.583 _____	6.038 _____	7.82 _____

Write the value of the underlined digit.

a	b	c
2. 0.3<u>1</u>4 _____	0.6<u>0</u>2 _____	0.07<u>9</u> _____

Write as a decimal.

a	b
3. fourteen thousandths _____	seven hundredths _____

Write each decimal in words.

4. 8.52 _____

5. 12.023 _____

Compare. Write <, >, or = in each blank.

a	b	c
6. 0.3 _____ 0.6	2.95 _____ 2.59	0.246 _____ 0.426

Write in order from least to greatest.

a	b
7. 0.53 0.32 0.42 _____	0.33 0.033 0.303 _____

Round to the nearest tenth.

a	b	c	d
8. 0.43 _____	0.75 _____	0.86 _____	0.98 _____

Round to the nearest one.

a	b	c	d
9. 14.6 _____	6.5 _____	19.8 _____	$13.44 _____

Write as a decimal.

a	b	c	d
10. $\frac{8}{100}$ _____	$\frac{72}{100}$ _____	$12\frac{72}{1000}$ _____	$2\frac{8}{10}$ _____

Write as a fraction or a mixed number.

a	b	c	d
11. 0.41 _____	0.017 _____	1.7 _____	0.03 _____

Addition of Decimals

To add decimals, line up the decimal points. Write zeros as needed.
Then add as with whole numbers.

Find: 5.7 + 6.84

Write a zero.	Add the hundredths.	Add the tenths. Regroup. Write a decimal point in the sum.	Add the ones.

T O Ts Hs
  5.7 0↙
+ 6.8 4
	T O Ts Hs
	  5.7 0
	+ 6.8 4
	       4
		T O Ts Hs
		  ¹
		  5.7 0
		+ 6.8 4
		   .5 4
			T O Ts Hs
			  ¹
			  5.7 0
			+ 6.8 4
			1 2.5 4

GUIDED PRACTICE

Add. Write zeros as needed.

	a	b	c	d
1.	T O Ts ¹ 1 2.7 +1 3.8 2 6.5	T O Ts 4 9.5 +2 7.3	T O Ts 3 4.6 +5 6.9	T O Ts 6 2.7 +1 4.5
2.	O Ts Hs Ths ¹ ¹ 1.2 4 5 +7.5 6 8 8.8 1 3	O Ts Hs Ths 3.5 1 8 +2.3 6 4	O Ts Hs Ths 7.0 0 5 +2.9 8 6	T O Ts Hs Ths 1 6.1 3 6 +4 8.0 5 4
3.	O Ts Hs $2.1 5 + 0.1 0↙ $2.2 5	O Ts Hs $8 + 1.7 8	O Ts Hs Ths 0.7 +0.5 6 5	T O Ts Hs Ths 4 3.6 3 7 +2 4.2
4.	T O Ts Hs ¹ ¹ 2.7 1 4.3 6 + 3.0 8 1 0.1 5	O Ts Hs 5.0 3 3.6 1 +0.9 5	T O Ts Hs 1.5 7.3 9 + 6.8	T O Ts Hs $ 6.4 7 2.8 9 3.1 5 + 1.2 4

114

PRACTICE

Add. Write zeros as needed.

	a	b	c	d	e
1.	5.7 +0.2	4.4 +2.8	4 2.9 +3 3.5	8.1 +9	4 6 +3 7.6
2.	1.3 1 +6.0 2	2.3 2 +1.9 6	2 4.2 7 +1 3.6 4	3.7 +4.0 4	0.6 9 +0.8
3.	$3 2.5 1 + 1 8.7 5	$6.3 2 + 3.4 2	$5 7.9 4 + 2 1.5 7	$7 4.1 8 + 1 0.5 2	$5.7 5 + 1.3 9
4.	0.6 4 9 +0.2 5 7	7.0 5 9 +3.1 8 6	6.8 +2.4 7 2	3 5.9 0 7 +1 5.6	4 5 +2 9.2 6 4
5.	1 6 5.3 +1 2 8.9	8 0.0 7 +1 8.6	0.8 9 +0.3 6	3.6 1 9 +2.3 2	5 4.9 +2 7.3 8

Line up the digits. Then add. Write zeros as needed.

	a	b	c
6.	0.9 + 0.6 = _____ $\begin{array}{r}0.9\\+0.6\\\hline\end{array}$	1.7 + 2.8 = _____	54.3 + 41.5 = _____
7.	$6.37 + $4.21 = _____	$0.23 + $8.76 = _____	$67.95 + $22.05 = _____
8.	8.815 + 0.173 = _____	4.321 + 9.876 = _____	2.843 + 1.562 = _____
9.	9.5 + 2 = _____ $\begin{array}{r}9.5\\+2.0\\\hline\end{array}$	14 + 3.2 = _____	0.6 + 16 = _____
10.	6.35 + 0.7 = _____	12.8 + 31.67 = _____	26.135 + 41.7 = _____

115

Add. Write zeros as needed.

	a	*b*	*c*	*d*	*e*
1.	6.9 4.6 +8.2	3.0 8 0.2 5 +2.5 4	7 4.8 5 6 4 3.4 2 9 +3 1.6 7 1	1.7 9 9.4 1 +6.8 6	2.5 6.7 +8.3
2.	3.8 7 +4.3	7.9 8.5 8 +9.4	6.4 8 0.6 +2	6.7 5 1 4.9 +3.3 5	1.5 8 8.0 2 7 +0.6
3.	$7.5 9.8 4.9 + 8.6	$8 5.2 7 6.7 8 3.8 + 1 0.4	$1 7.3 5 6 5.4 9 1 9.2 5 + 2 3.0 5	0.8 0.2 2 0.3 5 6 +0.4 3	1.5 0.5 0.2 5 +2.0 0 8

Line up the digits. Then add. Write zeros as needed.

a	*b*
4. 7 + 2.3 + 0.8 = _____	$5.74 + $8 + $1.46 = _____

7.0
2.3
+0.8

5. 1.4 + 4.5 + 8.9 + 6 = _____   7.86 + 3.7 + 7 + 4.423 = _____

■ MIXED PRACTICE ■■■■■■■■■■■■■■■■■■

Round to the nearest one.

	a	*b*	*c*	*d*	*e*
1.	8.3 _____	42.71 _____	16.625 _____	31.2 _____	9.521 _____

Round to the nearest tenth.

	a	*b*	*c*	*d*	*e*
2.	0.51 _____	1.65 _____	12.34 _____	7.861 _____	23.175 _____

DECIMALS AND MEASUREMENT

Estimation of Decimal Sums

To estimate decimal sums, first round the decimals to the same place. Then add the rounded numbers.

Estimate: $5.28 + $3.63

> Round each decimal to the nearest one.
> Add.
>
> $$\begin{array}{r} \$5.28 \rightarrow \quad 5 \\ +\ 3.63 \rightarrow +4 \\ \hline \$9 \end{array}$$

Estimate: 5.28 + 3.63

> Round each decimal to the nearest tenth.
> Add.
>
> $$\begin{array}{r} 5.28 \rightarrow \quad 5.3 \\ +3.63 \rightarrow +3.6 \\ \hline 8.9 \end{array}$$

PRACTICE

Estimate the sum by rounding to the nearest one.

	a	b	c	d
1.	$\begin{array}{r} 2.4 \rightarrow \quad 2 \\ +6.8 \rightarrow +7 \\ \hline 9 \end{array}$	$\begin{array}{r} \$5.0\,2 \rightarrow \\ +\ 8.1\,1 \rightarrow \\ \hline \end{array}$	$\begin{array}{r} 7\,2.6 \rightarrow \\ +3\,5.9 \rightarrow \\ \hline \end{array}$	$\begin{array}{r} \$4\,8.3\,5 \rightarrow \\ +\ 3\,7.6\,6 \rightarrow \\ \hline \end{array}$
2.	$\begin{array}{r} 7.8\,9 \rightarrow \\ +8.9 \ \rightarrow \\ \hline \end{array}$	$\begin{array}{r} 9.6\,5\,4 \rightarrow \\ +2.2\,1\,8 \rightarrow \\ \hline \end{array}$	$\begin{array}{r} 4.2\,7\,3 \rightarrow \\ +3.7\,9 \ \ \rightarrow \\ \hline \end{array}$	$\begin{array}{r} 2\,1.1\,0\,9 \rightarrow \\ +1\,8.3\,8\,1 \rightarrow \\ \hline \end{array}$

Estimate the sum by rounding to the nearest tenth.

	a	b	c	d
3.	$\begin{array}{r} 0.9\,3 \rightarrow \quad 0.9 \\ +0.2\,8 \rightarrow +0.3 \\ \hline 1.2 \end{array}$	$\begin{array}{r} 2.3\,1 \rightarrow \\ +4.5\,3 \rightarrow \\ \hline \end{array}$	$\begin{array}{r} 9.8\,8 \rightarrow \\ +\ 7.4\,3 \rightarrow \\ \hline \end{array}$	$\begin{array}{r} \$1\,2.6\,9 \rightarrow \\ +\ 8\,6.7\,6 \rightarrow \\ \hline \end{array}$
4.	$\begin{array}{r} 3\,8.5\,2 \rightarrow \\ +1\,4.6\,2 \rightarrow \\ \hline \end{array}$	$\begin{array}{r} 0.3\,8\,5 \rightarrow \\ +0.7\,6\,9 \rightarrow \\ \hline \end{array}$	$\begin{array}{r} 3.2\,6\,9 \rightarrow \\ +1.4\,1 \ \ \rightarrow \\ \hline \end{array}$	$\begin{array}{r} 5.7\,3 \ \ \rightarrow \\ +0.8\,9\,8 \rightarrow \\ \hline \end{array}$

Subtraction of Decimals

To subtract decimals, line up the decimal points. Write zeros as needed. Then subtract as with whole numbers.

Find: 28.3 − 14.95

Write a zero. Regroup. Subtract the hundredths.	Regroup. Subtract the tenths. Write a decimal point in the difference.	Subtract the ones.	Subtract the tens.

T O Ts Hs
2 10
2 8 . 3 0
−1 4 . 9 5
      5
	T O Ts Hs
	12
	7 2 10
	2 8 . 3 0
	−1 4 . 9 5
	    . 3 5
		T O Ts Hs
		12
		7 2 10
		2 8 . 3 0
		−1 4 . 9 5
		  3 . 3 5
			T O Ts Hs
			12
			7 2 10
			2 8 . 3 0
			−1 4 . 9 5
			1 3 . 3 5

GUIDED PRACTICE

Subtract. Write zeros as needed.

	a	b	c	d
1.	T O Ts 5 12 6 2 . 7 −1 4 . 2 4 8 . 5	T O Ts 8 3 . 8 −7 5 . 4	T O Ts Hs $5 3 . 8 2 − 1 0 . 1 1	T O Ts Hs $3 7 . 4 3 − 2 9 . 5 2
2.	O Ts Hs 9 7 10 10 8 . 0 0 −6 . 1 2 1 . 8 8	O Ts Hs 8 . 6 −4 . 2 9	T O Ts Hs 2 3 . 5 4 −1 2 . 6	T O Ts Hs 8 6 . 2 8 −5 4
3.	O Ts Hs Ths 6 10 4 12 7 . 0 5 2 −3 . 1 3 5 3 . 9 1 7	O Ts Hs Ths 6 . 2 3 8 −4 . 5 0 1	O Ts Hs Ths 1 . 5 2 5 −0 . 4 0 8	T O Ts Hs Ths 7 2 . 0 0 7 −6 4 . 1 6 9
4.	O Ts Hs Ths 10 8 11 0 10 9 . 2 1 0 −0 . 8 4 7 8 . 3 6 3	O Ts Hs Ths 7 . 5 1 6 −5 . 2 8	O Ts Hs Ths 1 . 9 −0 . 6 7 4	T O Ts Hs Ths 1 9 . 0 0 5 −1 4 . 5

Subtract. Write zeros as needed.

	a	b	c	d	e
1.	4.2 −2.4	1 6.5 −1 3.9	7.3 −0.8	9 −5.6	2 3.1 −1 2
2.	5.4 5 −0.1 6	0.9 6 −0.3 8	2 2.7 7 −1 1.8 8	7.0 2 −1.8	3 −2.6 2
3.	$6.2 8 − 2.6 4	$3.4 2 − 0.7 8	$1 7.6 3 − 1 3.4 5	$3 0.0 0 − 1 9.2 5	$2 4.9 5 − 1 2.6 5
4.	4.7 3 5 −1.3 2 3	5.7 1 5 −1.8 0 7	2 3.5 6 6 −1 1.8 4 5	2 1.7 3 −1 6.0 0 7	4 5.2 −2 8.9 7 6

Line up the digits. Then subtract. Write zeros as needed.

a	b	c
5. 9.6 − 3.7 = _____	7.02 − 1.86 = _____	4.007 − 2.628 = _____

$$\begin{array}{r} 9.6 \\ -3.7 \\ \hline \end{array}$$

6. 13.7 − 11.99 = _____   9.976 − 2.18 = _____   8.5 − 3.725 = _____

 MIXED PRACTICE

Subtract. Simplify.

	a	b	c	d	e
1.	$\frac{3}{5}$ $-\frac{2}{5}$	$\frac{7}{8}$ $-\frac{1}{8}$	$\frac{7}{10}$ $-\frac{1}{5}$	$2\,6\frac{1}{5}$ $-1\,4$	$1\,7$ $-\ \ 8\frac{5}{7}$
2.	$1\,2\frac{5}{9}$ $-1\,0\frac{1}{9}$	$9\frac{1}{12}$ $-4\frac{3}{4}$	$8\frac{1}{2}$ $-5\frac{3}{16}$	$2\,1\frac{5}{6}$ $-\ \ 7\frac{1}{3}$	$3\,2\frac{1}{8}$ $-1\,4\frac{1}{4}$

DECIMALS AND MEASUREMENT

Estimation of Decimal Differences

To estimate decimal difference, first round the decimals to the same place. Then subtract the rounded numbers.

Estimate: $8.93 − $6.29

Round each decimal to the nearest one. Subtract.

$$\begin{array}{r} \$8.93 \rightarrow\ 9 \\ -\ 6.29 \rightarrow \underline{-6} \\ \$3 \end{array}$$

Estimate: 8.93 − 6.29

Round each decimal to the nearest tenth. Subtract.

$$\begin{array}{r} 8.93 \rightarrow\ 8.9 \\ -6.29 \rightarrow \underline{-6.3} \\ 2.6 \end{array}$$

PRACTICE

Estimate each difference by rounding to the nearest one.

	a	b	c	d
1.	$6.1 \rightarrow\ 6$ $\underline{-2.8 \rightarrow\ -3}$ 3	$\$9.0\,7 \rightarrow$ $\underline{-\ 5.3\,5 \rightarrow}$	$1\,5.9 \rightarrow$ $\underline{-1\,1.2 \rightarrow}$	$\$4\,2.5\,7 \rightarrow$ $\underline{-\ 2\,7.8\,3 \rightarrow}$
2.	$7.4\ \ \rightarrow$ $\underline{-6.3\,4 \rightarrow}$	$3.9\,4\,4 \rightarrow$ $\underline{-1.3\,5\,1 \rightarrow}$	$1\,6.1\,7\ \ \rightarrow$ $\underline{-1\,0.6\,8\,2 \rightarrow}$	$3\,8.9\ \ \ \ \rightarrow$ $\underline{-1\,3.6\,6\,6 \rightarrow}$

Estimate each difference by rounding to the nearest tenth.

	a	b	c	d
3.	$0.8\,2 \rightarrow\ 0.8$ $\underline{-0.3\,9 \rightarrow\ -0.4}$ 0.4	$4.6\,4 \rightarrow$ $\underline{-\ 2.1\,3 \rightarrow}$	$2\,5.2\,7 \rightarrow$ $\underline{-1\,6.5\,1 \rightarrow}$	$3\,2.0\,8 \rightarrow$ $\underline{-\ 1\,9.7\,5 \rightarrow}$
4.	$4\,7.0\,2\,3 \rightarrow$ $\underline{-3\,9.3\,4\,5 \rightarrow}$	$5.3\,7 \rightarrow$ $\underline{-4.6\ \ \ \rightarrow}$	$6\,3.8\,7\ \ \rightarrow$ $\underline{-1\,0.1\,5\,4 \rightarrow}$	$9.2\ \ \ \ \rightarrow$ $\underline{-7.5\,9\,5 \rightarrow}$

PROBLEM SOLVING

Applications

Solve.

1. According to what insurance companies call a Life Expectancy Table, a ten-year-old child may expect to live 62.8 more years. How old would the person be then?

Answer _____

2. Before leaving on our trip, the odometer showed 4587.6 miles. We drove 314.7 miles that day. What mileage did the odometer then show?

Answer _____

3. A carload of bricks will average 37.31 tons. An average carload of lumber weighs 17.71 tons. How much heavier is the carload of bricks?

Answer _____

4. The winner of the hundred-yard dash ran the race in 11.6 seconds. The time of the second-place winner was 11.62 seconds. How much faster was the first-place time?

Answer _____

5. In June we received 8.9 inches of rain. In July we received 7.5 inches. How much more did it rain in June than in July?

Answer _____

6. Kurt had 5 gallons of gas in his car. He put in 9.8 gallons more. How many gallons did his car have then?

Answer _____

7. The butcher placed some meat on the scale. It weighed 1.4 kilograms. How much more is needed to make 2 kilograms?

Answer _____

8. Margaret rode her bicycle 10.75 miles one day and 8.25 miles the next day. How many miles did she ride in all?

Answer _____

Use a Bar Graph

A graph is a picture of data (factual information). A bar graph shows information in the shape of bars. Use a bar graph to answer questions about the data.

This bar graph shows the number of gold medals won at the 1976 Summer Olympic Games by six countries.

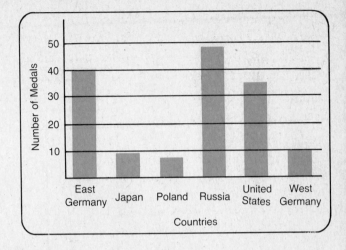

Read the problem.

How many more gold medals were won by Russia than by Poland?

Read the graph for data.

Use these steps when finding the needed data:

1. Locate the country on the horizontal scale along the bottom of the graph.

2. For each country, move to the top of the bar and back to the vertical scale along the side of the graph.

3. Write down the data.
   Data: Russia won 47 gold medals.
   Poland won 7 gold medals.

Solve the problem.

47 − 7 = 40
Russia won 40 more gold medals than Poland.

Solve. Use the bar graph above.

1. How many gold medals did Japan win in 1976?

   Answer _____

2. How many gold medals did the United States win in 1976?

   Answer _____

3. How many countries won more than 20 gold medals?

   Answer _____

4. How many gold medals were won by Japan and Poland together?

   Answer _____

5. How many more gold medals were won by East Germany than were won by West Germany?

   Answer _____

6. How many gold medals in all were won by the United States and Russia?

   Answer _____

PROBLEM-SOLVING STRATEGY

Use a Line Graph

A line graph may show how something can change over a period of time. The dots represent data (factual information). The lines connect the dots. Use a line graph to answer questions about the data.

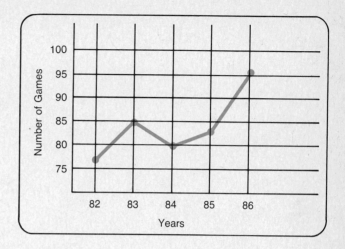

This graph shows the number of baseball games won by the Houston Astros over the five-year period from 1982 to 1986.

Read the problem.

How many more games did the Astros win in 1986 than in 1982?

Read the graph for data.

Use these steps when finding the needed data:

1. Locate the year on the horizontal scale along the bottom of the graph.

2. For each year, move up the line to the dot and back to the vertical scale along the side of the graph.

3. Write down the data.
   Data: Astros won 96 games in 1986.
   Astros won 77 games in 1982.

Solve the problem.

96 − 77 = 19
The Astros won 19 more games in 1986 than in 1982.

Solve. Use the line graph above.

1. In what year were the Astros most successful? Answer _____	2. In what year did the Astros win fewer than 80 games? Answer _____
3. How many times from 1982 to 1986 did the Astros win 80 games or more? Answer _____	4. How many games did the Astros win in 1985? Answer _____
5. How many games did the Astros win in 1983 and in 1984 combined? Answer _____	6. How many more games did the Astros win in 1983 than in 1982? Answer _____

DECIMALS AND MEASUREMENT

Metric Length: Meter and Kilometer

The meter (m) is the basic metric unit of length. A baseball bat is about 1 meter long.

A kilometer (km) is one thousand meters. (Kilo means 1000.) The kilometer is used to measure long distances. The distance from New York City to Chicago is 1140 km.

$$1 \text{ km} = 1000 \text{ m} \qquad 1 \text{ m} = 0.001 \text{ km}$$

The distance of a marathon race is about 42 km or 42000 m.
The altitude at which an airplane flies is about 9 km or 9000 m.
The width of a soccer field is about 68 m or 0.068 km.
The height of a soccer player is about 2 m or 0.002 km.

PRACTICE

How would you measure the following? Use m or km.

a   *b*

1. distance between cities _____   height of a jogger _____

2. perimeter of a garden _____   depth of a water well _____

3. length of a city block _____   distance to the moon _____

4. length of a river _____   length of an airplane _____

Circle the best measurement.

a   *b*

5. distance between airports   height of a ceiling

   125 m   125 km   2.8 m   2.8 km

6. length of six automobiles   distance walked in one hour

   30 m   30 km   6 m   5 km

Solve.

7. Owen drove 129.61 kilometers. Leo drove 138.64 kilometers. How much farther did Leo drive than Owen?

8. Sam jogged 3080 meters. Carlos jogged 2745 meters. How many meters in all did the two boys jog?

Answer _____   Answer _____

DECIMALS AND MEASUREMENT
Metric Length: Centimeter and Millimeter

A meter (m) can be measured with a meter stick.

A centimeter (cm) is one hundredth of a meter. (Centi means 0.01.) The centimeter is used to measure small lengths. Use centimeters to measure the length of a pencil.

⊢────⌐ 1 cm

A millimeter (mm) is one thousandth of a meter. (Milli means 0.001.) The millimeter is used to measure very small lengths. Use millimeters to measure the width of a fly.

⌐ 1 mm

| 1 m = 100 cm | 1 cm = 0.01 m | 1 mm = 0.1 cm |
| 1 m = 1000 mm | 1 cm = 10 mm | 1 mm = 0.001 m |

The height of a tree is about 11.4 m or 1140 cm.
The length of a pencil is about 19 cm or 190 mm.
The width of a housefly is about 5 mm or 0.5 cm.

PRACTICE

How would you measure the following? Use m, cm, or mm.

| | *a* | *b* |

1. width of your book _____   length of a small safety pin _____

2. height of a honeybee _____   length of your shoe _____

3. length of a basketball court _____   thickness of a penny _____

4. width of a pencil tip _____   height of a tree _____

Estimate the distance.

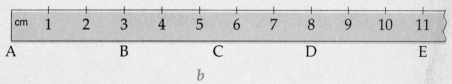

5. from A to B _____ cm   from B to C _____ cm

6. from A to E _____ cm   from C to E _____ cm

7. from B to D _____ cm   from B to E _____ cm

8. from C to D _____ cm   from D to E _____ cm

Solve.

9. Victor has 37 dominoes side by side. Each domino is 26 millimeters wide. What is the total width of all his dominoes?

10. There are 18 girls in a sewing class. Each girl needs 72 centimeters of ribbon to complete her project. How much ribbon is needed in all?

Answer _____   Answer _____

DECIMALS AND MEASUREMENT

Metric Mass

The word mass is not often used outside the field of science. The common term for mass is weight.

The gram (g) is the basic metric unit of mass. The gram is used to measure the weight of very light objects. A small paper clip weighs about 1 gram.

A kilogram (kg) is one thousand grams. It is used to measure the weight of heavier objects. Use kg for the weight of a dictionary. Remember, kilo means 1000.

$$\boxed{1 \text{ kg} = 1000 \text{ g}} \qquad \boxed{1 \text{ g} = 0.001 \text{ kg}}$$

The weight of an apple is about 45 g or 0.045 kg.
The weight of a dime is about 2 g or 0.002 kg.
The weight of a baseball bat is about 1 kg or 1000 g.

PRACTICE

How would you measure the following? Use g or kg.

          a   *b*

1. weight of a textbook _____   weight of a nickel _____

2. weight of a football _____   weight of a television _____

3. weight of a tack _____   weight of an orange _____

Circle the best measurement.

     a   *b*

4. weight of a dog   weight of a spoonful of salt

    9 g   9 kg   1 kg   1 g

5. weight of a loaf of bread   weight of a bicycle

    500 g   500 kg   18 g   18 kg

Solve.

6. A box of cereal weighs 504 grams. How many 28-gram servings are in the box?

7. Hans has a pair of shoes with a mass of 1.3 kilograms. He has another pair of shoes with a mass of 1.8 kilograms. What is the total mass of both pairs of shoes?

Answer _____   Answer _____

DECIMALS AND MEASUREMENT
Metric Capacity

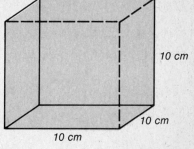

The liter (L) is the basic metric unit of capacity. A liter of liquid will fill a box 10 centimeters on each side.

A milliliter (mL) is one thousandth of a liter. It is used to measure very small amounts of liquid. A milliliter of liquid will fill a box 1 centimeter on each side.

Remember, milli means 0.001.

$$1 \text{ L} = 1000 \text{ mL} \qquad 1 \text{ mL} = 0.001 \text{ L}$$

A measuring cup holds about 250 mL or 0.25 L.
A small can of juice holds about 825 mL or 0.825 L.
A watering pail holds about 7.5 L or 7500 mL.
A ten-gallon fish tank holds about 38 L or 38000 mL.

PRACTICE

How would you measure the following? Use L or mL.

a | *b*

1. capacity of a tablespoon _____ capacity of a water jug _____

2. capacity of a bathtub _____ capacity of a medicine dropper _____

3. capacity of a milk glass _____ capacity of a teaspoon _____

4. capacity of a water pitcher _____ capacity of a cooking pot _____

Circle the best measurement.

a | *b*

5. capacity of a swimming pool

5000 ml   5000 L

capacity of a jug of apple cider

4 mL   4 L

6. capacity of a teapot

700 ml   700 L

capacity of a bowl

180 mL   180 L

Solve.

7. Pete wants to serve 14 glasses of punch. Each punch glass holds 245 milliliters. How much punch does he need?

8. A carton contained 2 liters of milk. Margo used 0.75 liters of milk from the carton. How much milk is left in the carton?

Answer _____

Answer _____

DECIMALS AND MEASUREMENT

Relating Units

You have studied some of the metric units in the table. The basic metric units are meter (m), liter (L), and gram (g). They are used with prefixes to form larger and smaller units.

For example:

- kilo- plus gram is kilogram (kg). Kg means 1000 g. Kg is larger than g.

- centi- plus meter is centimeter (cm). Cm means 0.01 m. Cm is smaller than m.

- milli- plus liter is milliliter (mL). ML means 0.001 L. ML is smaller than L.

larger

Prefix	Symbol	Meaning
kilo-	k	1000
hecto-	h	100
deka-	da	10
base unit	m, L, g	1
deci-	d	0.1
centi-	c	0.01
milli-	m	0.001

smaller

PRACTICE

Decide whether the following units are larger or smaller than the base unit. Then write < or >.

	a		b		c
1.	kL __>__ L		hm _____ m		dag _____ g
2.	cm _____ m		dL _____ L		mg _____ g
3.	kg _____ g		dam _____ m		mL _____ L
4.	dm _____ m		hg _____ g		cL _____ L

Give the value of each unit. Use the values in the table.

	a		b		c
5.	kL __1000__ L		cg _____ g		daL _____ L
6.	dg _____ g		hL _____ L		km _____ m
7.	dam _____ m		mm _____ m		cL _____ L
8.	hg _____ g		dm _____ m		mg _____ g

Decide which is larger or smaller. Then write < or >.

	a		b		c
9.	kL __>__ hL		daL _____ kL		hg _____ dag
10.	dg _____ cg		cm _____ hm		cm _____ km
11.	mm _____ dm		mg _____ cg		mL _____ hL
12.	dag _____ dg		kL _____ dL		dg _____ kg

128

Changing Units

To change from one unit to another, find the unit in the chart below. Move to the new unit. When you move right to a smaller unit, multiply by 10 for each step. When you move left to a larger unit, divide by 10 for each step.

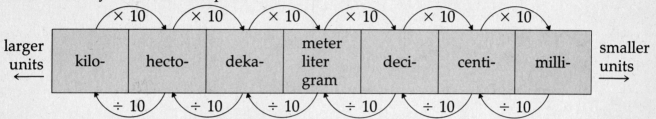

Find: 2 km = _____ m

To change km to m, find kilo- in the table. Find meter in the table. To change km to a smaller unit, multiply by 10 for each step.

$$2 \text{ km} = (2 \times 10 \times 10 \times 10) \text{ m}$$
$$= (2 \times 1000) \text{ m}$$
$$2 \text{ km} = 2000 \text{ m}$$

You will have more smaller units.

Find: 600 cm = _____ m

To change cm to m, find centi- in the table. Find meter in the table. To change cm to a larger unit, divide by 10 for each step.

$$600 \text{ cm} = (600 \div 10 \div 10) \text{ m}$$
$$= (60 \div 10) \text{ m}$$
$$600 \text{ cm} = 6 \text{ m}$$

You will have fewer larger units.

PRACTICE

Change each measurement to the smaller unit.

	a	b	c
1.	5 km = _____ m	95 m = _____ cm	32 cm = _____ mm
2.	62 L = _____ mL	17 hL = _____ L	853 L = _____ dL
3.	128 dag = _____ g	48 kg = _____ g	7 g = _____ mg

Change each measurement to the larger unit.

	a	b	c
4.	1700 mm = _____ cm	8200 cm = _____ m	57,000 m = _____ km
5.	3970 L = _____ daL	74,000 L = _____ kL	45,000 mL = _____ dL
6.	42,000 g = _____ kg	9000 mg = _____ g	100 hg = _____ kg

Select a Strategy

In this book, you have worked with several different problem solving strategies. Some of them are listed in the box at the right.

> **PROBLEM SOLVING STRATEGIES**
>
> Choose an Operation
> Make a Drawing
> Make a List
> Use Logic
> Use Estimation
> Use Guess and Check
> Work Backwards

Select a strategy from the box. Then solve.

1. Newschool is 450 yards east of Towncenter. Oldschool is 358 yards west of Towncenter. How far are Newschool and Oldschool from one another?

   Strategy _____

   Answer _____

2. Yoko has 43 stamps and 78 envelopes. She bought 20 stamps and 50 envelopes this morning. How many of each did she have before she went shopping today?

   Strategy _____

   Answer _____

3. Rolland has 4 coins. Their total value is 37¢. What coins does he have?

   Strategy _____

   Answer _____

4. Ken has $51 to spend on shirts. Shirts cost $11.25 each. Can he buy 5 shirts?

   Strategy _____

   Answer _____

5. The food manager at an amusement park ordered 432 boxes of hot-dog buns. If each box contains 12 buns, how many buns were ordered?

   Strategy _____

   Answer _____

6. Mike, Robin, and Cindy met at the swimming pool. One walked, one rode a bike, and one roller skated. Mike cannot roller skate. Cindy waved to Mike from her bike 10 minutes ago when he was crossing the street. How did each of them get to the pool?

   Strategy _____

   Answer _____

Unit 7 Review

Add. Write zeros as needed.

	a	b	c	d	e
1.	$1 4.9 5 + 2 7.3 8	9 0.7 +1 8.6	$0.8 9 + 0.7 4	3 6.1 9 7 +2 3.2 4 1	1 6 5.3 +1 2 8.9
2.	4.0 6 +2.3 8 7	2 3 4 +1 2 5.6 9	1 5.8 4 +2 3.7	2.2 0 2 +6.4	1 9.8 +1 6.0 7
3.	2 4.9 1 7.1 +1 3.8	7 0.6 5 3 4.1 5 +1 9.4	1 3.0 8 9 4 7 +3 5.2	2 1 5.0 6 1 2 2.1 8 +1 0 9.7	8.0 0 9 8.2 +7.3 6

Subtract. Write zeros as needed.

	a	b	c	d	e
4.	0.9 −0.4	$0.2 5 − 0.1 2	$2 2.8 0 − 1 4.2 0	0.0 8 9 −0.0 4 7	3 2 8.0 9 −1 6 4.6 4
5.	4.3 −2.3 8	1 9.8 4 −1 7.6	0.8 5 −0.8	6.5 −2.4 8	2 4 7.2 5 −1 9 1.3
6.	6 −0.3	3 4 −1 5.4	9 7.4 9 −6 8.6	4 5 3.1 7 −1 2 1.5	3 0 6.6 −2 1 9.1 2 7

Estimate the sum or difference by rounding to the nearest one.

	a	b	c	d
7.	9.6 5 +3.2	7.2 −5.4 6	2 8.3 +2 6.8 9	$6 0.2 5 − 1 9.3 0

Estimate the sum or difference by rounding to the nearest tenth.

	a	b	c	d
8.	0.7 8 +0.1 2	7.4 6 − 3.2 8	3.6 4 5 +2.8 9	8.3 −6.5 7 4

Unit 7 Review

Circle the best measurement.

	a	b

1. length of a crayon   mass of a leaf

     9 cm   9 m   1 g   1 kg

2. capacity of a waste basket   height of a room

    30 mL   30 L   2.4 cm   2.4 m

3. mass of a cat   height of a mountain

    8 g   8 kg   8.8 m   8.8 km

4. width of a postage stamp   capacity of a juice glass

   20 mm   20 cm   150 mL   150 L

Change each measurement to the smaller unit.

	a	b	c
5.	7 m = _____ cm	19 km = _____ m	14 g = _____ mg
6.	8 L = _____ mL	1 m = _____ mm	5 kg = _____ g
7.	15 cm = _____ mm	44 cm = _____ mm	1 L = _____ mL

Change each measurement to the larger unit.

	a	b	c
8.	4000 g = _____ kg	370 mm = _____ cm	230 mm = _____ cm
9.	600 cm = _____ m	2000 mL = _____ L	3000 m = _____ km
10.	12,000 mg = _____ g	7000 g = _____ kg	9000 mm = _____ m

Solve.

11. Jesse Owens jumped 8.06 meters in the long jump competition of the 1936 Olympics. In 1984 Carl Lewis jumped 8.54 meters. How much farther did Lewis jump than Owens?

Answer _____

12. The Merrimack River is about 180 kilometers long. The Mississippi River is about 21 times as long. About how long is the Mississippi River?

Answer _____

Write the place name for the 5 in each number.

      a   *b*

1. 852,067 _____   8,943,573 _____

Write each number using digits. Insert commas where needed.

2. four hundred sixteen thousand, seven hundred twelve _____

3. two million, five hundred ninety-four thousand, three _____

Compare. Write <, >, or =.

    a   *b*   *c*

4. 90 _____ 48   509 _____ 509   72 _____ 86

Round to the nearest hundred.

    a   *b*   *c*

5. 758 _____   921 _____   2044 _____

Add.

	a	*b*	*c*	*d*
6.	829 +159	8788 +9853	3,624 +27,569	619,724 + 21,449

Subtract.

	a	*b*	*c*	*d*
7.	238 − 89	1121 − 632	650 −269	83,019 −71,821

Line up the digits. Find each answer.

    a   *b*

8. 855 − 59 = _____   46 + 351 + 523 = _____

Estimate the sum or difference.

	a	*b*	*c*	*d*
9.	725→ +936→	809 +939	3850 − 278	9058 − 646

	b	*c*	*d*
2 3 × 9	4 2 6 × 5	1 3 0 7 × 8	2 6,1 7 3 × 4

11.

| 7 5
×3 7 | 7 0 5
× 4 2 | 1 1 2
×2 2 3 | 8 0 3
×3 5 4 |

Divide.

a	*b*	*c*	*d*

12.

8)2 5 0   2 2)8 7 6   3 1)2 7 2 9   6 0)3 6,9 0 0

13.

7)5 4 1   4 1)6 7 3   4 9)5 3 4 1   2 7)8 5 8 6

Estimate the product or quotient.

a	*b*	*c*	*d*

14.

8 5 →   2 6   7)6 4 0   4 5)3 2 5
×1 9 →   ×2 4

Solve.

15. A railroad boxcar can carry 1540 bushels of wheat. If a bushel of wheat weighs 60 pounds, how many pounds of wheat can the car carry?

16. Terrence has 672 stamps to put into his album. He can put 32 stamps on each page. How many pages does he need?

Answer _____

Answer _____

Add. Simplify.

	a	*b*	*c*	*d*
17.	$\frac{2}{11}$ $+\frac{5}{11}$	$\frac{3}{8}$ $+\frac{1}{8}$	$3\frac{1}{7}$ $+6\frac{4}{7}$	$8\frac{4}{9}$ $+7\frac{2}{9}$
18.	$\frac{2}{3}$ $+\frac{1}{6}$	$\frac{9}{10}$ $+\frac{2}{5}$	$8\frac{1}{9}$ $+2\frac{3}{18}$	$6\frac{3}{4}$ $+3\frac{1}{8}$

Subtract. Simplify.

	a	*b*	*c*	*d*
19.	$\frac{10}{13}$ $-\frac{6}{13}$	$\frac{15}{16}$ $-\frac{9}{16}$	$16\frac{11}{12}$ $-\ \ 4\frac{5}{12}$	$35\frac{5}{6}$ $-29\frac{1}{6}$
20.	$\frac{5}{6}$ $-\frac{1}{2}$	$\frac{3}{4}$ $-\frac{1}{12}$	9 $-3\frac{3}{10}$	$8\frac{1}{5}$ $-1\frac{3}{10}$

Change each measurement to the smaller unit.

	a	*b*	*c*
21.	9 ft = _____ in.	$2\frac{1}{2}$ lb = _____ oz	$5\frac{1}{3}$ yd = _____ ft
22.	4 T = _____ lb	8 pt = _____ c	12 qt = _____ pt

Change each measurement to the larger unit.

	a	*b*	*c*
23.	72 in. = _____ yd	6 qt = _____ gal	48 oz = _____ lb
24.	9 c = _____ pt	5000 lb = _____ T	30 in. = _____ ft

Solve.

25. James lives $\frac{3}{4}$ mile from school. Sam lives $\frac{1}{2}$ mile from school. How much farther from school does James live?

Answer _____

26. Ruth wants to build two shelves. One is to be $3\frac{1}{3}$ feet long and the other is to be $4\frac{2}{3}$ feet long. How long a board does she need for both shelves?

Answer _____

Write the place name for the 6 in each number.

        a   *b*   *c*

27. 13.65 _____   0.076 _____   4.26 _____

Write as a decimal.

                a   *b*

28. nine and eight hundredths _____   thirty-one thousandths _____

Compare. Write <, >, or =.

        a   *b*   *c*

29. 8.035 _____ 8.35   2.8 _____ 2.80   0.562 _____ 0.522

Round to the nearest tenth.

        a   *b*   *c*

30. 10.12 _____   6.55 _____   0.87 _____

Add. Write zeros as needed.

	a	*b*	*c*	*d*
31.	5.6 2	8.4	6.7 0 3	$7 5.2 4
	+8.9 6	+4.6 1 9	+2.9	+ 8 4.8 3

Subtract. Write zeros as needed.

	a	*b*	*c*	*d*
32.	6.3 6	4 7.7	9.0	$4 4.8 7
	−0.7 9	− 3.4 8	−2.8 3 6	− 2 7.6 1

Change each measurement to the smaller unit.

        a   *b*   *c*

33. 9 kg = _____ g   2 L = _____ mL   54 m = _____ cm

Change each measurement to the larger unit.

        a   *b*   *c*

34. 300 cm = _____ m   1000 mL = _____ L   6000 g = _____ kg

Solve.

35. Dee Massalas bought a briefcase on sale for $54.50. The original price was $65. How much did she save?

36. From Planta to Otis Junction is 17.4 kilometers. From Otis Junction to Villita is 14.5 kilometers farther. How far is it from Planta to Villita?

Answer _____   Answer _____